THE MURDER OF GABBAR

THE MURDER OF GABBAR

VENKAT RAMAN V

Anecdote
Publishing House
For the love of quality reading!

Anecdote
Publishing House
For the love of quality reading!

anecdotepublishinghouse.com
champreaders.com

Anecdote Publishing House
2nd Floor 2/15 Lane no. 2 Ansari Road, Daryaganj-110002
Email: info@anecdotepublishinghouse.com
Website: anecdotepublishinghouse.com

Published by Anecdote Publishing House

First Edition 2025
ISBN 978-81-973806-7-9
MRP ₹ 350

Book Promoted and Marketed by Champ Readers Pvt. Ltd.
Edited by Meraki
Cover design by The Book Bakers
Layout by Graphic Tailor
Printed by Thomson Press (India) Ltd, New Delhi

CONTENTS

AUTHOR'S NOTE

This book would never have happened if not for my father. He has been carrying me in his heart from the moment my mother had me in her womb. While my mother supported me, my dad kept pushing me. Every success of mine, I owe it to them. Eternally grateful for the blessing that is my parents. Upon turning 30, I started the Venkatachalam-Kalyani (VK) Scholarship with Deepam Charitable Trust in their honour. I will need several lifetimes to thank them properly. This is just a start.

Every writer needs readers. I had great friends who read my pathetic early attempts at writing and continued to give great feedback. I thank each and every one of my friends and relatives for encouraging me to keep writing and being lovable critics.

I came across Suhail Mathur as a writer during the covid pandemic. I did not know then that he ran The Book Bakers literary agency. When I first spoke to him, he was every bit as positive as those he represents say he is. He helped me get a deal for this book and one more (at the time of this writing). I've got half-a-dozen manuscripts waiting for him to help me launch. He's been a great friend and an excellent mentor.

Sincere thanks to Anecdote Publishing for taking an interest in my book.

To Jane Borges (Mafia Queens of Mumbai) and Bhaswar Mukherjee (The Counterfeiter). Thank you for guiding me during the deal signing process. They had very little reason to help me but they did with an open heart. For that, I'll always be grateful.

And finally, to warriors.

Ours is the first civilization to revere women. We had Gods in the female form and we had a hierarchy that placed the woman above all else. *Mata Pitha Guru Deivam* (Mother, then father, then the teacher and finally God). Yet, society continues to be difficult to navigate for women. Among the many crimes against women, rape is the worst. It is brutal, inhuman and deplorable.

A rape is not a woman's fault. She never asks for it. Yet she goes through it. It is not just rape. Sexual crimes are on the rise. Every person who fights these crimes is a warrior. They need our support, not our judgment. A rape is the fault of the rapist alone. This book is for those warriors and their families.

PREFACE

7:30 PM

"Hello," said the female voice nervously.

"Hello," replied the man confidently. Not many people had this number. If they called this number, they were calling for one thing only. The call was from a private number. That was not unusual.

"I was told I could call this number if I wanted to finish…to get…" began the female voice but struggled to find the right words.

"What do you want done and when? Our services are discreet and the best," said the man quietly. He knew to use the right words. They ran a hit squad but their calls were handled professionally.

"I…" began the voice nervously.

"Speak freely," said the man quickly.

"I want three people killed. I want it done as soon as possible," said the woman.

"Three?" the man asked with surprise. While the caller sounded nervous, three was a big number, even for their city. "Who do you want killed?" he asked sharply.

"Gabbar and his two bodyguards," said the woman in a nervous voice.

"Gabbar? You mean Baaji's son?" the man asked. This was not the first time they had gotten a call to finish Gabbar. There had been two other calls in the past week. There was a long silence.

"How much can you pay?" the man asked doubtfully.

"Fi-Fifty thousand rupees," said the woman.

The man rolled his eyes. "You must be joking. Have you been living under a rock? You need ten times that amount for a normal person. Gabbar is a powerful man. Fifty thousand! Are you kidding me?" he shouted.

As he finished speaking, the call ended. The man shook his head, but smiled. The woman had no idea about the current rates. Crime was not cheap. As he sat thinking, he got another call. This time, it was not from a private number. He answered the call nevertheless.

"We are calling from … bank. Do you need a personal loan?" a female voice asked.

"Damn you!" the man shouted and ended the call. The phone network followed them everywhere. So did the loan peddlers.

***

1:45 AM

Gabbar was a lot more drunk than usual. His vision was blurred and he had a faint idea of where he was. When sober, he knew this area like the back of his hand. That day, he had had too much even by his standards. He staggered forward. Most people had gone to bed. A few people had the habit of sleeping outside their homes during this season. Apart from their snoring and the chirping of crickets, the only sound was that of the ocean. He looked around, unsure of where he was. He decided to walk towards the direction of the sound of the ocean. He would know where he was after reaching the main road by the ocean.

Anyone else would be afraid to go to the deserted road at this time of the night but Gabbar was the reason for their fear. He was the king of the area. Within a few minutes, he reached the main road. He was walking towards the left where his house was when he sensed some movement behind him.

He turned around, looking for the source of the slight sound of movement. He could see a white figure walking away from him at some distance.

"Why, you little..." he said, looking bemused. There were rumours about the marina at night and he wanted to finish this once and for all. He increased his pace, seeing the distance between them. He was gaining on the white figure when he slipped and fell face-first onto the ground. He felt something hot on his face.

He touched the spot and looked at his finger. There was blood on it. He swore loudly, got to his feet and broke into a sprint. As he closed in on that person, he figured it was a woman in white clothes. He grabbed her shoulder and grinned. The woman turned and his grin faded.

There was a dull thud and everything went black.

CHAPTER 1

A DEATH IN THE MARINA

7:45 AM

The alarm rang loudly as he woke up with a start. He looked at the phone and realised that he had already snoozed the alarm nine times. He always had trouble waking up. With his family on vacation, this became a habit. He was usually woken up much earlier by his wife. He rolled over and began to stretch to warm himself up. He looked at his phone and saw that there were more than thirty missed calls.

"Hello dear," he said as he returned the call.

"Hey Dad," said his eldest son, Rishi, answering the phone.

"I was hoping to talk to your mom," said Gaurav, stifling a yawn.

"She gave me the phone around five calls ago. She got tired of trying to wake you," said Rishi, laughing through the words.

"Tell her I am sorry," he said as he walked towards the bathroom.

"Mom told me that you would say that. She told me that she sent you messages scolding you," he said, laughing hysterically.

"I know. Shouldn't be any different from the usual," said Gaurav as he began to chat with his son about his day.

"Dad, we spoke for an hour last night. I have only slept since then," said Rishi, sounding bored.

"I have to make the best use of your vacation. We don't get to talk much when you are here," said Gaurav, looking at his phone. He noticed that half the missed calls were from the deputy commissioner. "I'll call you back in sometime," he said quickly to Rishi and cut the call. The deputy commissioner never called him since he had requested to be transferred from law and order.

"About time," said the deputy commissioner, picking up the call at the first ring.

"I haven't spoken to you in a long time," said Gaurav warmly.

"No time for niceties. I want you to come to the abandoned port in the west of the marina right away," said the DCP in a serious, no-nonsense tone.

"I will be expected in—" began Gaurav nervously.

"Everything has been arranged with your superiors. I wanted you here twenty minutes ago. Hurry up," he said and abruptly ended the call.

Gaurav dressed quickly and drove towards the marina. He had transferred out of law and order three years ago, and worked with the governor's security detail now. He had been promoted to the rank of Deputy Superintendent of Police only a few months before asking to leave. The position and pay were good but he had grown tired of dealing with criminals and being in sticky situations. The job was not exactly risky but it affected him more than he cared to admit. More importantly, it affected his family life.

There are many policemen in this country who put their duty above their family. Gaurav Singh was not one of them. There had been a time when he had been like that but all that had changed. He had two kids who were growing up and he chose to put them above the job. Gaurav wasn't the best fighter in the force. He couldn't handle gangs of goons alone but he had a speciality. He knew how to negotiate a compromise among criminal gangs.

Criminal gangs were always looking for an excuse to fight with each other. One random act of violence could often trigger a war. Gaurav made few arrests and even fewer convictions but he could keep crime and violence in check in sensitive situations. That helped the police protect the innocent. It was not something that grabbed headlines but it was essential. The DCP had been very disappointed when he had asked for a transfer right after being promoted. He had been a trusted ally to the DCP, who had refused to even meet him all this while, not for the lack of efforts on Gaurav's part.

The governor's security detail was a dull job but it had one upside. It had less risk and almost no violence. He worked proper hours and the job seldom demanded more than that from him. He was required to be available on call round the clock but this governor was so low-key that half the people did not even know his name. Proper hours meant that he could spend more time with his children.

It also came with other perks. His marriage had been going through a turbulent period. He refused to take bribes but the officers around him did not. His wife, Sunitha, did not understand or agree with his reasoning. She argued that if the rest of them were doing it, he must too. One of the main reasons he got the job at the governor's office was because nobody wanted it. There was almost no scope for making something on the side. While his income did not change, she was satisfied because he was spending more time with the family.

Memories of the time since he left the DCP flashed in his mind during that drive. He reached the marina in twenty minutes. He parked his bike and stretched for a few seconds. He had a quick look at the mirror to adjust his moustache. One he was satisfied with it, he took a look around. There were a lot of people who had gathered around the area. Policemen were trying to ensure that people did not step into their perimeter. He quickly walked up to the policeman by the barrier who gave him a quick salute as he stepped in. He gave him directions to the crime scene and continued to manage the crowd.

One look at the crowd told Gaurav all that he needed to know. Someone important had been attacked or killed. The west of the marina area belonged to Rajan Bhai. Rajan Bhai was a politician now and a stalwart of the ruling party. He was favoured by an influential minister and the party gave him the protection he needed from the police. While Rajan Bhai remained the political face, his older brother Baaji was the muscle. Baaji was now fifty years old but everyone in the city knew to fear the name. Police seldom came to this area. If they were closing the area, something big must have happened.

This was the section of the marina where old and damaged fishing boats were abandoned. The whole area smelled of rotting fish but the area had another purpose—it was close to the port and was used to smuggle goods out of the port. If you needed anything smuggled out of the port, Baaji was your man. What started with just electronics had expanded to so much more over the last two decades. Everyone knew this but nobody intervened. Every political party and several businessmen had interest in the area. Baaji and Rajan Bhai had a profitable operation and they made sure there were no rivals.

Gaurav quickened his pace and saw a red police jeep parked close to the beach sand. Standing near the jeep was the DCP and a few policemen.

"About time, Gaurav," said the DCP loudly. The DCP was bald and clean-shaven. That hid his age effectively. He was leaning on a pole and rolling his eyes. His large eyes made him look more menacing than he actually was.

"The traffic was bad," said Gaurav sheepishly as he walked closer.

The other policemen walked away on cue. "I know you wanted a quiet life but I had no other option here," said the DCP, showing him a body.

There was a body of a spread-eagled man a few feet away. The man was cut and bruised in many places and part of his face looked like it was smashed with a stone. The body had been outlined and several objects around the body had been marked for evidence. The forensics team was waiting at a distance for the DCP to let them resume their work.

"How can I help? You seem to have a big team involved in this," said Gaurav softly.

"Look at his face," said the DCP.

There was a lot of blood as the face was caved in but it did not take Gaurav long to identify the body. The man on the ground was Gabbar. He was Baaji's son. He ran a few operations for his father and there were speculations that he would take over the entire operation when his father retired. Gabbar was a very aggressive kid. Gaurav remembered him from years ago. He feared nobody, not even the police.

"This is bad," said Gaurav in disbelief.

"This is a catastrophe," said the DCP.

"What do you expect me to do?" Gaurav asked.

"You know what I expect," said the DCP pointedly.

"Nobody can do what you are going to ask me to do," said Gaurav.

"I know, but I have no choice," said the DCP.

Gaurav used to be an expert in negotiating with criminal gangs in the city. He knew most of them and they trusted him. Moreover, they respected him. That was something that most policemen could not claim. There were many policemen who opposed gangsters and there were those who were in cahoots with them and happily accepted bribes. The criminals despised the first kind and did not respect the other. Nobody could do what Gaurav did. That made him unique.

What people did not understand about controlling crime was that criminals would exist, no matter what. Crime was an industry. Business, politics and so much more depended on it. There was no way to completely eradicate it. The best way to deal with crime was by keeping it under control. It was like the cockroach under the drain. Everybody knew that it was there but as long as one did not see it, it did not exist.

Gaurav was one of the people who had been responsible for keeping crime in check. The key was to identify what the gangs wanted and get them to talk it out. Arranging such conversations was not something any random officer could achieve. He could get the gangs together, get them to talk and convince them to arrive at a compromise. It was his speciality.

When he had been with law and order, he was the person who constantly negotiated peace between different criminal gangs. He once negotiated a truce that kept the city from entering into a state of emergency. He kept crime in check and minimized damage to the public, with his first priority being the safety of civilians. The higher authorities were also fine with crime on the ground level. They did not want too much attention on it. As long as it did not attract the public attention, they were happy. Gaurav used to be the first person on the scene in most crime cases.

He had done this many times. It was not easy to do what he did. Crime lords were more willing to lose money than lose face. The negotiation was all about satisfying egos. Gaurav had diffused many issues of the sort but none of them involved a brutal murder of someone as important as Gabbar.

"This is impossible," said Gaurav.

The DCP sighed. He only had two more years of service before he retired. He had been hoping for a promotion before retirement but he knew that it was a lost cause. He neither had the favour nor the influence to get that promotion. He had convinced himself to have a quiet couple of years but this murder was going to give him many sleepless nights.

"We still have to try and do something quickly. The body count otherwise will be unimaginable," said the DCP gravely.

There were two major gangs in the city. Rajan Bhai and his brother ran the smuggling operations in the west marina area. The other was Akhtar, the oldest of all the gangsters. Akhtar did not believe in politics. He was still on the streets and it was a matter of pride to him. Akhtar was the most violent of all the bosses and he liked to make a spectacle of his crimes. He was almost as smart as Rajan and as fearless as Baaji.

Akhtar had two businesses. The first was Hawala and the other was drugs. He was responsible for more than fifty per cent of all Hawala transactions in the state. His business made him important to every dirty politician. The police knew not to interfere with his business. Many were also on his payroll.

There were smaller gangs and the most important person among the smaller gangs was Cyrus. Against the commonly seen transition from crime to politics, Cyrus did the opposite. His father had been a politician. He had moderate success but he was murdered by one of his enemies. That was one of the most talked about murders in the state. His father was starting to make a name and was one of the favourites for the upcoming elections when he was killed. He was decapitated and displayed in public. The police could not find anything about the murder. There was no arrest and the case is still open.

Cyrus wanted to take revenge and became a feared ruffian in the city. He ran the markets. The central market in the city was the place from which grains and vegetables were sold in bulk to the whole state. There was a lot of money in it. He had taken over the place and settled in. Rajan Bhai had the west marina, Akhtar occupied the downtown area and Cyrus had the markets. While Cyrus had a very small operation, he controlled a large area comparatively. Between these three gangsters, they owned most of the city. There were other gangsters but they were either unimportant or lackeys to one of the two major bosses in the city.

Rajan Bhai and Baaji had a lot of enemies. The nature of their business made that unavoidable. There was hardly anyone who they had not angered. Policemen, politicians and businessmen all had a bone to pick with them. However, nobody had enough guts to attack them directly. Rajan was very smart and equally powerful. Baaji was brash but he knew enough to trust Rajan. Rajan ensured that they were almost never implicated in their illegal activities. His greatest nemesis was Akhtar.

Akhtar had a personal beef with Rajan Bhai. Rajan's wife, Nasreen, was Akhtar's sister. Almost fifteen years ago, word had spread that she had been kidnapped. It was during the early days of Gaurav's career when he had joined as a sub-inspector. All hell had broken loose and Akhtar had his men roaming the streets, attacking anyone from Rajan's gang on sight. Just when both the gangs were about to clash head-on, Nasreen and Rajan had proclaimed their love for each other.

Akhtar could not make his sister a widow but he disowned her that instant. They never spoke to each other since then. Rajan and Nasreen were still together but Akhtar never forgave them. He did not bother to visit even when Nasreen had two children. There were rumours that he had a bounty on their heads. The bounty was still a topic of conversation among gang members in bars, and over time, rumors had inflated the sum.

It was three years after this incident when Cyrus lost his father. Nobody knew who killed him but word on the street was that a politician had offered a seat to whoever would kill him. The offer was made to every gangster in the city, including Akhtar and Rajan. There was no information on whether they did it but members of both gangs often credited themselves for that murder. Rajan joined politics but in a different party and Akhtar never spoke about it.

Cyrus killed the politician who made the offer but the man had taken the name of the killer to his grave. He spent a short time in jail for this murder but he had won the case due to lack of witnesses. He used every opportunity to hurt Rajan and Akhtar but neither of them took him seriously. He still had no idea who killed his father and he was not strong enough to significantly hurt them yet.

Baaji had four children. Gabbar was his eldest and he had three daughters after him. His wife had died a few years ago and Nasreen was like a mother to all the children in the house. Nasreen and Rajan had a nine-year-old daughter and a six-year-old son. Baaji's eldest daughter was married to a politician and the other two daughters were still studying.

Gabbar was twenty-seven years old and he was being groomed to take over the business. Rajan treated Gabbar like his own son. Rajan and Baaji lived in a large house on the edge of the marina. They had their ninety-year-old aunt living with them. Rajan had set up several shell companies and businesses which acted as fronts to launder the money he made illegally. He had a loyal team who made this operation seamless. Rajan was feared but he was trying to build a positive image for his political career. He was naturally charismatic and his posters were all over the city.

Gabbar was brash and aggressive. His combat skills would probably be sung about in folklore. He had every bad habit in the book but never got into the crosshairs of the police. He had more enemies than his father and uncle combined and a few of his enemies were from their own gang. This made his murder an even bigger headache for the police. Anyone could have killed him.

Every person in the city was a potential suspect. Rajan and Baaji were gangsters but they had a very good image among their followers and the public in their area. They were like heroes.

Unlike his father and uncle, Gabbar had almost no goodwill. The manner of his death was brutal. He had several cuts on his body and a portion of his face had been caved in using a heavy stone. He had been killed a few hours after midnight based on the initial estimate of the medical team. There were no bodies of any of Gabbar's men. That was the most surprising aspect of all this. Gabbar was seldom alone. Even when he visited questionable places, his men always stood guard. He had been attacked and there was no trace of the others.

"Where are his men?" Gaurav asked.

"They were all arrested last night for a drunk driving incident. They let Gabbar go free as they did not feel like holding him," said the DCP.

"Typical," said Gaurav sarcastically.

"Would you have handled it differently?" the DCP asked, looking irritated.

"It doesn't matter, does it? What is done is done. Was Baaji informed?" Gaurav asked.

"He and Rajan are on their way. I didn't want civilians nearby," said the DCP.

"You were first on scene?" Gaurav asked.

"I wish! The IG called me three hours ago about this. Prabhat Mishra, the head constable in this area, called him personally. Looks like he wanted to show off to the IG's office. The idiot! He left me looking like a fool when I answered the call," said the DCP.

"Who handles this area now?" Gaurav asked.

"There is a sub-inspector but he is on medical leave. He met with a minor accident a few days back. I've asked him to come in. Unless they are bedridden or dead, I want everyone here. This is going to be bad so I wanted you. I've cleared it with your superiors. Help me in this case and you can go back to your beloved governor," said the DCP.

"For how long do I have the crime scene?" Gaurav asked, looking around. He knew that he would not have much time on the scene if Rajan was on his way. He would have photos and other samples but nothing could be as helpful as being on the scene in murder cases. He wanted to make sure he had enough time to observe the crime scene.

"You would have had it for a few minutes if you had taken my call. I can't keep the family away any longer. Rajan is putting a lot of pressure on me as it is," said the DCP.

"I have not even had a proper look," said Gaurav in protest. He had not even examined the body properly. He wished he had woken up a little earlier.

"They have taken enough pictures. Feroz is heading forensics. He does a good job but keep this in mind—I did not call you here to solve this case. I don't know how quickly we can solve this or if this can be solved at all. Catching the killer in this case won't matter. Don't be surprised if someone surrenders to take the blame. I am more concerned about keeping violence under control," said DCP.

"That's right. You have better investigators. You want me to do the impossible," said Gaurav with a sigh. He knew that the DCP would not have called him if he did not have any other option. While he hated being here, he knew that this was inevitable. It was only a few days but this was important. This was a catastrophe that made him throw away his personal reservations. He could not fathom how much violence this would cause across the city. If left unchecked, this could escalate exponentially. Whatever happened, he was not going to have any sleep for the next few days. On the bright side, working on this case could repair his relationship with the DCP.

"I guess I have to cancel my leaves now," said Gaurav sadly as they walked back to the jeep. He regretted the timing of the murder. His wife was her best self during vacations.

"I hear that you chase crows in the governor's office. Why would you want to take a break from that?" the DCP asked with a smirk.

***

Ajmal smiled as he ended the call. He was told horrifying details about a murder in the marina but he did not feel bad about it. He could not help grinning and sat on the chair with a look of satisfaction on his face.

"What did you do?" Shaheena asked as she spotted him.

Ajmal's grin widened. He did not need to say a word. He only wished that he could see Baaji's face now.

CHAPTER 2

RAGE OF GANGSTERS

Gaurav made sure to speak to the team on the ground. He knew most of them from his time here. They knew the seriousness of the situation and did not hesitate to obey him. He wanted them to control the public and avoid any violence on the scene. They were now waiting for the ambulance to take the body away. For some reason, it was getting delayed. As he stood waiting, he saw a large number of cars approaching the scene.

Rajan and Baaji were in the first car but they were closely followed by a dozen vehicles filled with their gang members and family. Rajan was the first to get out of the car. He was tall and had pronounced features. He had neatly trimmed facial hair and looked very handsome. He had a grim look on his face but he looked strong effortlessly. He opened the door for his brother, who stepped out with a grave look on his face.

Baaji was shorter than his brother but stockier. He had a scar just below his left eye and had a small paunch but that did not make him any less menacing.

While Rajan looked charming at first glance, Baaji was intimidating. One by one, the other cars came to a halt. In a matter of minutes, there were a few hundred people around the scene. Baaji's daughters were wailing loudly and had to be held by others as Gaurav and the DCP walked towards them.

The DCP immediately shot a worried look at Gaurav and he moved instinctively. Rajan and Baaji were fine but Gabbar's body was not in a condition for his family to look at. They had to limit the number of people who saw the body. The sight of the body alone could trigger violence.

Baaji looked furious as he saw Gaurav advance but he made the rest of them wait. He came forward, closely followed by Rajan. They looked menacing and Gaurav swallowed hard as he slowly moved towards them. Gaurav looked back uneasily but the DCP was already on his way to help him. He waited as the DCP crossed him and walked to Rajan. He looked nervous himself but took a deep breath and faced the brothers.

"Patel Saab, you people have the nerve to stop us from seeing our boy?" Rajan asked menacingly. He looked angry but his eyes were red. He was putting on a brave face but he looked shaken.

"Sir, the women…it would be unwise to let them see him like this," said Gaurav slowly, trying to convince Rajan. He knew that Rajan would not listen to them unless he knew that the police were on his side.

Rajan's anger vanished. He realised that Gaurav was making a valid point. He held Gaurav's hand awkwardly. "DSP Gaurav, I haven't seen you in a while," he said.

"I got a transfer. I don't work in this area anymore. Please sir, his sisters should not see him like this," repeated Gaurav as he saw the girls advance. Rajan looked at Gaurav and then nodded at his men. The men immediately stayed back, holding the family members while Rajan attempted to go forward. Gaurav walked in front of him and tried to look apologetic. "It is not a pleasant sight, sir," said Gaurav softly.

"Stay here, Baaji. Come with me, Gaurav Saab," said Rajan. The DCP came with them quietly as they walked towards the body. They walked slowly as the rest of them waited impatiently. Baaji ignored his brother and followed them with three men behind him. Gaurav was dreading this moment.

As tough as Baaji was, he was not prepared to see his son in this condition. He had been looking tough all this while but he broke down before they reached Gabbar's body. He dropped to the ground, banged his fists on the ground and howled in pain. Rajan turned and looked at his men. As though they had read his mind, two men came to help Baaji. Baaji had to be restrained. His fists were bleeding from punching the ground but his rage had taken over him.

Rajan Bhai continued to look at Gabbar's body. Unlike his brother, he was calm. He crouched next to the man and looked closely. He closely observed each wound. His eyes welled up but he looked stoic. His lips were pursed and he focused on each wound like he was a policeman. He stretched his hand and almost touched Gabbar's forehead.

"I am sorry, sir. This is a crime scene. You cannot touch him," said the DCP firmly.

Rajan stared at Gaurav but did not disobey him. He nodded and stood up. "I want you guys to finish the formalities and hand over the body to us as soon as possible. Put pressure on whomever you want. Use my name wherever necessary. Call me at any time if someone stalls you. I know you have your procedures but make him presentable for his funeral. Baaji's son cannot be seen like this," said Rajan quickly.

"Sure, sir. Definitely," said the DCP politely.

"Once you hand him over, I want you to report only to me. I don't want any arrests regarding this. No press or anything of the sort. We will deal with this," said Rajan gravely.

"Sir, I cannot let you—" began the DCP in protest.

"Look here, Patel Saab. You don't let me do anything here. This is my city and this is my area. Someone laid a hand on my family. There will be blood. A lot of it. I am giving you a warning. Don't mistake this as me seeking your permission. My men will find whoever is behind this and their death will come in the papers very soon. It will be brutal. Much more than this. Until then, I want you to stay out of our way," said Rajan menacingly.

Rajan turned and walked away, leaving the policemen bewildered. They looked at each other helplessly. This was not going to end well. "This is bad," said Gaurav as Rajan walked away.

"You think?" the DCP asked sarcastically and rolled his eyes.

"He wants to start a war. We have until the funeral to work something out with him. If we don't do something until then…" began Gaurav.

"I know. Do what you have to do. I will make sure you get whatever you want. We have very little time. Rajan might be pissed off now but he is a smart man. He will cool down. I am more worried about Baaji," said the DCP, looking worried.

"Let me start talking to people and identify the best way to deal with this," said Gaurav, twirling his moustache absent-mindedly.

"Don't let me down. I am counting on you," said the DCP.

Gaurav walked away, deep in thought. He was thinking about ways to approach this case. He did not have much to work with and he had very little time to figure things out. Rajan had not said the words but he had declared a war in front of them. They were late but in a case like this, there was no way to be early. He had already gained some goodwill from Rajan but he wondered if that would make a difference. This was a nightmare.

Gaurav spent the next hour coordinating with the DCP. They had to control the area immediately. They had every policeman who was on leave called to the area. They had also requested for additional forces from nearby stations to help contain the situation. By that evening, they had four patrol cars and thirty-six police constables assembled in the area. The men were asked to move around in pairs or groups of three as a precaution. The whole area was sensitive and almost anything could trigger violence. The people of the area were not new to attacking policemen.

Gaurav spent most of the day instructing them on the details of the area while going over the crime scene photographs. He knew that he would not get any sleep that night. He made the calls and asked for the case files to be sent to his home. He knew that the DCP had told him to concentrate on diffusing the situation but solving the case was a good way to do that.

The DCP got a riot specialist temporarily assigned to the area. He knew how to control violence with violence. He was running a few drills and passing instructions to the men as Gaurav left the area. Gaurav spent a lot of time that night going through the case files. The reports were better than he had expected. Feroz had been thorough and he had covered larger ground than Gaurav would have.

However, the evidence was inconclusive. There were several different unidentified blood samples in the area. Gabbar had moved quite a distance between the point where he had first been attacked and the point where he had died. Someone had taken their time to kill him and nobody had heard a thing. If gangsters in the city planned something like this, they knew how to do it clean. High-profile murders were usually quick and clean. If it was a brutal crime scene, it was meant to be that way.

This was brutal but not exactly a spectacle. If someone wanted to make a statement, there were more efficient ways to do it. Then again, this was Gabbar. He was not easy to subdue. He was six feet tall and weighed almost ninety kilograms. He could hold his own against three men and his mere presence was intimidating even to policemen. There was evidence that showed he had fought back. Even drunk, Gabbar was dangerous.

The timing of the murder was a clear indicator that the murder was planned. Whoever killed him was either incredibly lucky or knew that Gabbar would be exposed and vulnerable at that time. Gaurav did not believe in luck. This was planned but not by a professional. This was done by someone who knew where Gabbar was at all times.

He made a mental note to question the officers who had arrested Gabbar's entourage. While what they had done was normal, it could not be a coincidence that they had been held and Gabbar had been released alone on the day when he was killed. He realised that they would have to be protected as Rajan Bhai's men could blame them if a killer was not found. He made a mental note to get them temporary protection.

The choice of location was more confusing. People could not come into the marina area just like that. There were eyes everywhere and Rajan was informed about everything. If anyone had seen anything, Rajan would know. Despite his position as a gangster, Rajan had the loyalty of most of the residents of the area. Someone had closely followed Gabbar and taken their chance. The tussle had not been clean. Gabbar had fought back. There were too many different blood samples in the area. Either the witnesses were waiting to tell Baaji or this was an inside job. The chatter on the street was non-existent and the only thing they heard was that every gang was going on the defensive.

"Whoever hurt Gabbar must have had something personal against him," said Gaurav to himself. There was evidence of a struggle. There were marks of strangulation around his neck but Gabbar had not died quickly. It was the blows to his head that killed him, though he had been hurt all over his body. Gabbar looked like he had been beaten long after he was dead. His killer knew where he would be and when he would be at his weakest. It wasn't easy taking this man on but it had been done. This was a carefully planned but awkwardly executed murder. Or it was made to look that way. The location helped the killer. Based on what the police had so far, the killer had a good chance of walking away from this.

Gaurav spent time trying to reconstruct the events of the previous night. Nothing seemed out of the ordinary. Feroz had put the time of death two hours after midnight. Gabbar had taken the route he used less often to go home. That was the only way this could have happened. Nobody could confront Gabbar anywhere else in the marina. There were people around all the time. There was a police check-post where Gabbar had been stopped. The police had done the customary check. Every person in that car was drunk.

Gabbar usually drove an imported MUV. At least five other people had been there with him. The patrol officers had called the sub-inspector in the local station about the situation. That person was Iqbal Siddique who had been on leave. He had contacted his superiors regarding the matter. Within fifteen minutes of the capture, the patrol officers were asked to hold the car, release Gabbar and keep Gabbar's companions in the station overnight. No charges were filed.

Gabbar had been isolated from his men at around two hours past midnight. He had walked back into the area. They had not been able to determine the exact path but there were a few witnesses who gave the police an idea of the route taken. Many people in the slum area had the habit of sleeping outside their homes. A few had seen him but they were unsure about the time as they were mostly asleep.

After a point, there had been no people that day in his route. The last person to see him was convinced that the time was half-past one in the morning. Instead of going home, Gabbar had taken a detour. Gabbar had walked with a bottle in his hand towards the ocean. Somewhere in the next half hour, he had been murdered.

"When will the reports be ready?" Gaurav asked a member of the forensics team who was on duty. He hated to disturb the people who worked the graveyard shift but he had to get the details at the earliest.

"I can give you the post-mortem in three hours," said the man, sounding annoyed.

"You are Ananth, right? We worked on the triple murder in the plaza," said Gaurav, trying to establish a rapport. He recognised Ananth and he was glad that he knew the man. He could get his reports hurried.

"Yeah, I remember. I haven't seen you around here in a while," said Ananth calmly as he got his tools ready.

"I moved to a different department," said Gaurav.

"Good for you. I have been trying for ten years to get out of dealing with dead bodies," said Ananth calmly.

"When will the reports be ready?" Gaurav asked.

"I told you already. I will give you the post-mortem in three hours," said Ananth indifferently.

"The DNA samples around the body?" Gaurav asked.

"Possibly never. Have you seen this place? This is a cesspool of DNA. I see more than thirty different samples on the body and not everything is blood. I don't even know if half the things here are human. There are dead dogs, fish and possibly so much more. I'll do my best but we don't have the manpower to catalogue so many items," said the man frankly.

"What? We need the samples. I can get the DCP…" began Gaurav.

"Gaurav, I have known you long enough. If you are here, they are not looking to find a killer. They want this case closed smoothly. I'll do what I can but this is a lot. I am one man and this is the first time I am working nights in seven months," said Ananth.

Gaurav smiled awkwardly. His fame preceded him. Ananth had heard about him. While it was disappointing to hear his response, it was true. His speciality was closing cases smoothly. He almost exclusively handled sensitive cases.

This case had happened in the marina, which was Gabbar's area. It was a murder that looked like it was done by an amateur. No person had come forward with information to the police or Rajan Bhai. If he had received any information, there would have been violence. Time was running out and they had to find something quickly.

***

8:00 AM (THE NEXT DAY)

"Can you give me a quick summary of the body, the injuries and so on?" the DCP asked. The DCP had come to his temporary workplace in his old station. Unexpectedly, Rajan had come with him. Gaurav looked uneasily at Rajan and then at the DCP. The DCP widened his eyes but there was nothing he could do.

"Go on. Tell me who hurt my boy and how," said Rajan commandingly.

Feroz looked at the DCP and swallowed nervously. "Speak freely. It is not like you did this," said Rajan sharply. He pursed his lips and stared straight at Feroz.

"This was done by one or two men. They caught him by surprise. This was not just a contract kill. The wounds look personal. While they caught him by surprise, this was done by inexperienced people who had underestimated Gabbar. The problem is, we have too much DNA. I even found semen around him although I don't think that had anything to do with this murder," he said and looked nervously at Rajan.

"Go on, Officer. You are only telling us what happened. Tell us the full story," said Rajan but he looked stoic. It was hard to say whether he was angry or sad.

"He has more than twenty cuts on his upper body, his right knee was broken and I suspect multiple fractures. None of these are clean. There was a sharp stone nearby. I think his head was bashed in using that stone but he was beaten with many objects," said Feroz. Rajan closed his eyes and hissed. His emotions were more visible now. He was battling anger and sorrow but kept a straight face. Feroz hesitated but continued, "I will know more once I take the body to the lab. I will give you more information later," said Feroz.

"Did he suffer much?" Rajan asked, folding his hands and looking up.

"Sir, you don't need to…" began Gaurav, trying to sound considerate.

"I must know…" said Rajan seriously.

"He was alive the entire time. His face was bashed in. Sir, I don't want to lie to you. He suffered a lot. Please do not ask me the details. It will only grieve you more," said Feroz, sounding polite.

Rajan smiled weakly. He nodded as Feroz left the spot. "Patel Saab! When you notify the press, I don't want the news coming out that Baaji's son was killed by just one person. Your reports must back that too. As far as the rest of the world is concerned, my boy was ambushed by a group of ten men at least. I want him referred to as an activist in your statement. I will handle the media but make sure that you do not call him a criminal. There has been no case against him and I want it to remain that way. I don't care who you pin this on. Your investigation is an eyewash. The minister will want you to close this soon and keep it low-key. I want you to oblige him," said Rajan.

Gaurav looked at Rajan with disbelief but the DCP nodded uncomfortably. Once Rajan was far away, the DCP sighed and shook his head. "He has the nerve to order me around," he said and spat on the ground. He took his cap off and ran his hand over his bald head slowly.

"Why do you take this crap from him?" Gaurav asked.

"You know why. If I refuse to take crap from him, he will ensure that someone else does it worse to me," said the DCP.

"Why me? I know you told me that you want me on this case but you have plenty of capable officials under your command," said Gaurav.

"I am not sure about that. I might have better investigators but not many people consider consequences and none of them are discreet. You are different. You don't want press conferences or the limelight. You are exactly who I need," said the DCP appreciatively.

"What are you expecting from me?" Gaurav asked.

"While I hate agreeing with Rajan, the actual case is second priority. The whole city has been disturbed by this and it could get very violent very quickly. Rajan's gang is thirsty for blood and revenge while the other gangs will see this as an opportunity to strike. I want you to ensure that the violence does not come to the streets," said the DCP.

"It is going to be very difficult," said Gaurav.

"Not for you. This is your forte. It is difficult for the rest of us. Despite not being here for a while, you still know the streets better than most of us. You would not be here if I did not believe that you can handle this," said the DCP encouragingly.

Gaurav sighed. He had lost most of his contacts and his rapport with them. Even if he had the contacts, this was extremely difficult. With an issue as sensitive as this, he could afford no mistakes.

CHAPTER 3

HAPPY WIFE, HAPPY LIFE

9:30 AM

The newspaper had been read many times already that day. The front page had been plastered with a headline that read 'Activist Killed in the Marina'. The woman reading the paper did not recognise the name mentioned. It was that way for most of the city. The murder victim was better known as Gabbar. As she read the paper, her lips curved into a smile. She read the article thrice to get the details memorised. *Good riddance*, she told herself as she leaned back on her chair. As the words escaped her mouth, she realised that she was in a room full of people. Everyone was staring at her. Almost everyone looked afraid. She did not care. She only hoped that Gabbar had suffered enough.

One woman walked up to her slowly. She smiled politely and gestured to ask for the paper. The woman who had spoken aloud gave the other woman the paper.

"A lot of us think the same. We just don't say it out loud," said the other woman in a whisper. She looked down at the woman and smiled again reassuringly. As she turned around, the embroidery on her bag was clearly visible. It read 'Angel'.

"We can go now if you are ready," said a familiar voice. While the sudden voice gave her a jolt, she knew who it was. The woman turned to face a man whose presence calmed her. She smiled weakly and walked towards him.

***

10:15 AM

"You are not coming?" Sunitha asked, sounding disappointed.

"I cannot. The DCP called me in. Baaji Bhai's son was murdered and they want me to come back to law and order for this case," said Gaurav calmly to his wife.

"I understand. I know that you won't avoid this unless you have no other choice. I want you to stay safe. Do you want me to come there? I can leave the kids here and take the next bus if you want," said Sunitha, sounding sincere.

"I'd love to see you but this is going to be a bad couple of weeks. I will hardly be home and I don't even know what kind of hours I will be working. We both don't need to suffer. Stay there. Enjoy the break with the kids. I know your mom must be pampering you," said Gaurav truthfully.

"She has me eating like I am pregnant. I'm going to be fat when I come back," said Sunitha, sounding girlish.

"You will always be beautiful to me," said Gaurav, knowing well that this was exactly what she expected him to say. She liked it when he said things like this. Gaurav did not mind saying it. It made her happy. When she was happy, she made him happy too. As he ended the call, he remembered how they had come to be this way.

Gaurav had met Sunitha a few months after he first got his appointment as a sub-inspector. Their parents knew each other and the decision was made for them within an hour. They were married three months later. What followed the honeymoon was a very sweet period, but very soon, she grew frustrated with Gaurav. He was a strict disciplinarian at work and refused to take bribes. He also spent most of his time at work. He was kind to her and he treated her well but he had his own moral code which she did not understand. She was tired of seeing people who worked for her husband take bribes and live luxuriously. Before she could tell him this openly, Rishi was born.

After returning to the city after her delivery, he could sense that she was distant. Talking about it did not help. Sunitha was like a mob-wife. She did not care how he got the money as long as he got it for her. Her wishes could not all be achieved with his salary. In another three years, they had another son and named him Raghav. While she took good care of him and their children, Sunitha had become even more distant. He spent very little time at home and they were still living in the police quarters.

She took their children and went back home when he said that he could not afford the school that she wanted. This was after almost eight years of their marriage. Gaurav's parents had passed away by then and his sister had moved abroad. She and their children were all that he had.

Sunitha's father had told him before his marriage to set aside a part of his salary and give it to him for safekeeping. He had been doing that religiously but he never asked the old man any questions. While he went to her house to convince her to come back, he understood why. He knew Sunitha's nature. The old man had saved his money wisely and there was a sizeable sum in his name now. That along with the tiny sum his father had left him was almost enough to get their own house in the city. He advised Gaurav to promise Sunitha that they would get a house and even vouched for him when she refused to believe him.

She came back with him and slowly became normal. By the time she had returned, he had applied for the governor's detail job. Perhaps it was meant to be. The job came just after a promotion and also gave him a pay revision. At the same time, he got a contact from a bank who told him about a property auction. He only had to take a small loan to get a decent house in a good locality. Another contact in the governor's office got his children admitted to a good school which charged less fees. With that, Sunitha became more loving than she had ever been to him.

The school did wonders for his kids. Both his kids were extremely good at academics and Sunitha spent most of her time enrolling and training them for contests. She never compromised on caring for him. Giving her what she wanted only made her care more for him. They became close to each other and understood each other much more than before. His father-in-law had saved his marriage. He had doubled the amount that he sent his father-in-law since that incident. He had no idea what his life would have been if not for that man.

Gaurav had coffee to bring his focus back to the case. He was sitting in the meeting room to work undisturbed. He knew that he did not have much time. He had to start thinking of ways to contain this situation. He hardly had any time to inspect the crime scene properly. There was nothing useful in the crime scene to give them a lead. The place was a hub of all undesirable activities. There were too many prints on the rock used to bash Gabbar's head in. There were around a dozen blood samples surrounding the scene from different periods based on the reports. They were still waiting on the coroner's report but it wouldn't make a difference. Gaurav knew that this case was not about detective work. It was about damage control. Gaurav sighed as he closed the files. He had nothing.

"Stop sleeping, Gaurav," came a stern but familiar voice.

The DCP walked towards him. Walking beside him was a man with a sling around his right arm and a few bandages on his face. "This is Siddique. He is the sub-inspector whose leave I cancelled. Take him with you. You can use my driver, Krishna, for this period. Krishna will be there at your beck and call at any time of the day," said the man. Without so much as an introduction, he turned and walked away.

"Good afternoon, sir," said Siddique, trying to salute.

"What do I call you?" Gaurav asked immediately.

"They call me Siddique," said the man eagerly. He was clean-shaven and his uniform was crisply ironed. He was not tall and he had an erect posture.

"Alright, Mr Siddique. Don't bother with the salute. Are you healthy enough to work?"

"Just a hairline fracture. This is an emergency," said the man eagerly.

Gaurav smiled awkwardly and turned away. The man was young and over-enthusiastic. The man clearly saw being called from his leave as an honour. He made a mental note to involve him as little as possible. The man's face was still bruised and he looked like he needed a week's rest to return back to normalcy.

"Just to set the expectations straight, priority is to contain the situation," said Gaurav.

"We are not catching the killer?" the man asked, looking surprised. He had a peculiar expression on his face as he spoke the words.

"The first priority is to stop a gang war," said Gaurav importantly.

"I will help in any way that I have to," said the man seriously.

"Get ready. We need to leave in five minutes. Any information you get from the streets is welcome. Our priority is to stop violence before this becomes a full-blown war," said Gaurav, running his fingers over his moustache.

"Sure," said the man, reaching for his phone.

Siddique made his calls as Gaurav walked towards the parking area. The DCP had given him his car. He did not need the car but he appreciated the gesture. His current driver kept proper hours. He also needed someone who knew the area well. He looked around for the vehicle and spotted it but there was no driver near it.

"Have you seen Krishna?" he asked Siddique but the man was out of earshot, talking on his phone. *Just brilliant*, said Gaurav to himself.

"Good morning," said a well-built young woman

in a police uniform as she gave him a quick salute.

Gaurav wished her as he dialled the DCP reluctantly. He was yawning frequently. He snapped his fingers and shook his head to focus. He felt sleep deprived and he was less effective when he was sleep deprived. He had been told that a driver would be waiting for him. There was no network coverage in the parking area. He had a lot of work to do. The last thing he wanted to do was to call the DCP and locate the driver.

"Good morning, Sir," said the woman again. She raised her chest up high and gave him another salute.

"Good morning," said Gaurav curtly and moved a few feet to get a signal on his phone. He had no idea who the woman was and he had no time to chat.

"The DCP sent me," said the woman, following him.

"I don't think so. I was only told that I would be getting a driver. We never spoke about a policewoman," said Gaurav quickly.

"I am Krishna," said the woman, saluting him once again.

Gaurav was surprised. The woman was possibly in her late-twenties. She was muscular and tall. Her presence was intimidating. She looked at him with a smirk. She was used to people expecting a driver to be a man and she seemed to be enjoying the misunderstanding. "You are Krishna?" Gaurav asked slowly.

"I get that a lot. My name confuses people. I drive for the DCP from time to time. I work for the highway patrol unit as a driver," said the woman with a smile.

"Oh, I'm sorry I didn't..." said Gaurav, stopping for a minute. He wasn't sure if he should complete the sentence.

"Don't worry about it, sir. I'm used to it. People expect a man when they hear my name," she said with a grin. She was enjoying this conversation.

"Siddique, let's go," said Gaurav quickly, calling out to the man. He did not want the awkwardness to continue.

"Shouldn't we wait for Krishna?" Siddique asked, looking around.

"This is Krishna. She works for the DCP," said Gaurav with a weak grin. At least, he wasn't the only one to make the mistake.

Krishna turned around the car smoothly, grinning the entire time. It seemed as though she wanted to show Gaurav that she could drive very well. "Where to?" Krishna asked as she brought the car to a perfect halt.

"You really get this a lot, don't you?" Gaurav asked as he sat in the car.

"It has always been like this," she said as Siddique got into the car.

"I've checked with my people. Most of them are just hearing about this. There are a couple of people I would like to go directly to. They must have an idea about how this happened," said Siddique as he got into the car.

"Where do you want to go first?" Gaurav asked.

"There's a small shop near the slum at the marina. The shop sells smokes and whatnot and has a lot of people that come and go. The shopkeeper hears about anything and everything that happens in the area. If something happened to someone in the area, that is where you get the information," said Siddique.

Gaurav knew the place. This was the right way to begin work on this case. Gaurav nodded at Krishna and nudged his head towards Siddique. The SI began to give directions as Gaurav immersed himself in thought. He was thinking of the possibilities. There were too many suspects and too little time. He was expected to stop a gang war that had most likely begun already. He had been out of this line of work for a long time now. He usually knew what each gang wanted from the other. That helped negotiate in meetings such as these. He had nothing this time. He had to gather information and he had to do it very quickly.

The shop at the end of the marina was a place of buzzing business. The shop was small but the revenue it generated was immense. They opened before sunrise and did not close till midnight. The owner was someone who grew up with Baaji. He had started this when Baaji had begun to run the streets with Rajan. All they sold was tea and snacks but the shop's revenue could rival several big hotels in the city. On an average, there were about a dozen customers at all times. In addition to this, they sold cigarettes and whatnot.

The owner of the shop owned an entire compound with around twenty houses. He had acquired it over the years. He could survive on the rent alone but he continued to do what he had done over the years. One of his sons followed him to the shop but his other three sons had businesses of their own. The little shop had six people employed and they did not close on any day.

In addition to being frequented by police, gang members and civilians alike, the shop had a good vantage of the entire marina. The owner and the people working in the shop knew everything there was to know about the marina. Hardly anything could happen without their knowledge. They knew where their loyalties lay. They said nothing that could harm Baaji or anyone related to him. Police knew not to pressure them as they were spoken for. They gave them enough tips to maintain good terms. These tips were usually cleared with Baaji or Rajan but were still useful. Baaji was known to frequent the shop. The owner was a polite man. As Gaurav knew the man, he was recognised immediately.

"I haven't seen you here for a long time now, Sir," said the man respectfully.

"I moved to a different department," said Gaurav as he acknowledged him.

"What would you like to have? The samosas are fresh. You must have some," he said as he snapped his fingers. The closest attendant began to lay a few snacks on a plate.

"No. Please. Not now. I will be back for it. I will just take a tea now," said Gaurav with a warm smile.

"Chotu!" the owner called a tall boy who was making tea. The boy was wearing a gold chain and rings. Gaurav guessed that this was his son. "Let us take a walk with this nice man," he said pointedly to the boy. Gaurav gestured to Siddique to follow him.

"This is one of my sons. He is the only one who is not too proud to come to the shop," he said, patting the boy on his back. "This is Gaurav Sir. He is a senior officer," said the man proudly to his son. The boy nodded curtly and forced a smile. He quickly excused himself and went back to the shop. The owner walked further away for a minute. "I assume this is about Baaji's boy," said the man gravely.

"I'm afraid it is," said Gaurav.

"Terrible. He was an angry young man but he was always polite to me. He could never have enough of my snacks," said the man fondly. There were no tears in his eyes. "Every kid in this area eats what I make at some time or the other. I remember almost all of them. You would think you would be used to death by now," said the man, shaking his head.

"You have seen that many people die?" Siddique

asked with surprise.

"You don't live too far away from here. You are a policeman in this area. You tell me," said the owner rhetorically. "I have become used to death. It comes with this area. It is cursed. Watching these kids die is one thing but to see your best friend lose his son is worse. No father should have to watch his kid die. Definitely not in this way," said the man sadly.

"I know you don't speak to us regarding cases unless…" began Gaurav doubtfully.

"It doesn't matter in this case. I spoke to Rajan Bhai already and I know who did it," said the owner.

"Who?" Siddique asked, looking at the man with shock.

"Bhadra," said the man indifferently.

"No way," said Siddique and Gaurav together. Siddique looked at Gaurav with surprise.

"I used to work in this area," said Gaurav pointedly.

Everyone in the marina area knew that name. Bhadra was a female ghost, clad in a white saree that many people saw in the marina area. There were several origin stories surrounding Bhadra. Some claimed that she was the ghost of a woman who was killed by a scorned lover. Others claimed that she was a sort of bloodsucking devil. A lot of people claimed to have seen Bhadra roam in the marina at times.

The rumour had existed for decades and people saw Bhadra very often. Everyone ignored the fact that most of the people who saw her were drunk. Some people even worshipped Bhadra. Whenever someone saw Bhadra, they were taken to their respective places of worship to rid themselves of the evil. Gaurav had never given the story much thought but Siddique looked like he was partially sold on it.

"That night, Gabbar chased her. A few people saw him following a woman clad in white. Which woman in her right mind would roam the marina so late in the night? He tried to play with Bhadra. He tried to play with the devil. Bhadra is not forgiving. The vengeful woman killed him," said the owner.

This was another common thing among the youngsters. Kids used to dare each other to walk the marina at night. Many kids even fainted during these dares. Gaurav couldn't understand why Gabbar would chase Bhadra. Gabbar was no little boy but Gaurav made a mental note that Gabbar was drunk.

"A lot of you people believe that she isn't real. I assure you. She is real. She is not human," said the owner seriously.

Gaurav spent a little more time talking to the man about a few other things. He knew what to say and what not to say. Gaurav could tell that the man was being honest when he was speaking about Bhadra. That was why he had no qualms discussing this. He did not give straight answers on any other topic.

"How vulnerable does this make Rajan?" Gaurav

asked, slowly moving away from Siddique. He knew that the owner could give him an answer if he wanted. He folded his hands and looked at the owner directly.

The man took a long look at him. "Gabbar was like a son to Rajan. I often felt that he loved Gabbar like his first-born. That doesn't change anything. Rajan is who he is. He is shaken but it would be foolish to think that he is weak," said the owner.

"The men?" Gaurav asked doubtfully.

"They know who leads them. If I had to go up against Bhadra or Rajan, I would choose Bhadra. Does that answer your question?" the owner said seriously.

Gaurav thanked the man and walked to the car quickly. "What do you think of the killer? Do you think this makes sense?" Gaurav asked sarcastically as they left the marina.

"I have been in this area my whole life. I still don't know whether the stories are true," said Siddique.

"They are stories and you are a policeman. Don't tell me you believe in ghosts," said Gaurav, laughing at him.

"If you are talking about Bhadra, she is real," said Krishna. Both men turned to her immediately.

"You know about Bhadra? I thought you weren't from around here," said Gaurav.

"The whole city knows about Bhadra. So many people have seen her. It was on the news," said Krishna. She looked surprised that Gaurav was dismissive of the idea.

"That doesn't make it true. Bhadra is a story. People have been using the story to suit their narrative over the years," said Gaurav.

"If Baaji believes this, there will be no violence. He can't chase a ghost and we can all relax," said Siddique calmly.

"Yeah. I can go back to my department and take that leave that I had applied for," said Gaurav fondly. Siddique did not understand the sarcasm. "Pigs can fly," added Gaurav sarcastically to make his point. The whole discussion had gotten them nowhere. Gaurav had hoped that something good would come out of this. He shook his head as he realised that he had to question the one person he had hoped never to meet again.

CHAPTER 4

AN AGEING LION

2:20 PM

An hour after their talk, they were in Akhtar Bhai's area. Gaurav remained silent as he got memories of an incident from seven years ago. He began to look outside as the event flashed in his mind.

"Where are we going now?" Siddique asked.

"He is not a suspect but there's just something I want to check," said Gaurav. He walked into the area, looking around for a specific house. He remembered this area far too well for his liking. He looked at the house and it was exactly as he remembered. The kitchen window faced the front and he saw a woman washing vessels. She did not notice him immediately but once she did, she came out rather fast.

"I knew you would come here when I heard the news," she said in a whisper.

"How are you doing?" Gaurav asked calmly as he sat at her doorstep. Siddique had followed Gaurav but remained silent.

"We are good. We have been safe," said the woman nervously. She kept looking at Gaurav but frequently glanced at Siddique.

"What about Aman?" Gaurav asked reluctantly.

"He is working in Ahmedabad in a factory," said the woman slowly.

"He went so far away from home for work?" Gaurav asked, rubbing his moustache and looking at her doubtfully.

"I insisted. If he was here, he could do something stupid. I sent him away soon after he finished school," said the woman. By then, the passers-by had noticed a couple of men questioning her. They paused in their tracks to stare and listen in but walked away when Gaurav looked at them.

"Where is he now?" Gaurav asked.

"In Ahmedabad. He only comes here twice a year and I make sure that he does not stay for long. I don't expect him for another couple of months. I don't want him getting into any trouble," said the woman, looking worried.

"He is well?" Gaurav asked.

"He is occupied. He does not have time to think of anything else," said the woman.

"Where was he—?" Gaurav began awkwardly.

"In Ahmedabad. He was at work," said the woman immediately.

"If he is there, what are you doing here?" Gaurav asked.

"He hardly makes enough for himself. I work as a maid in a few houses near the area. Once he settles down, I will go there as well," said the woman.

"I will need details of his place of work and his stay. I will also need to speak to him," said Gaurav in a low voice.

"Please, we have been living away from—" began the woman nervously.

"It will just be me. I won't let anyone else know. I will talk to him and you won't hear from me again," said Gaurav immediately.

The woman hesitated. She looked uneasily at Siddique. She quickly got her phone and showed it to Gaurav. She made sure that it was hidden from Siddique's view. She held Gaurav's hand and looked at him with fear. Siddique wondered what was going on but chose to remain silent.

"Stay safe. I told you to get out of the city at the earliest. This was always a temporary solution for you. If you need help in any way, reach out to Das. He will know how to find me," said Gaurav as he noted down the details she had shared on a small paper. He carefully folded it and kept it in his pocket.

"Who was that?" Siddique asked after they had come far away from the house.

"She is one of the main reasons I left this unit," said Gaurav gravely.

"Were you and—?" Siddique began awkwardly. He

felt like he had asked a question that he should not have asked.

"Nothing like that. My image in the department is not just for show," said Gaurav.

"Who is she?" Siddique asked.

"Do you remember Soren?" Gaurav asked in a whisper.

"I have not seen him but I have heard the name somewhere," said Siddique, trying to recollect the name. He shook his head after a few seconds.

"Soren was Baaji's henchman. You would not have heard anything about what happened to him because it was meant to be that way. It was the hardest case that I worked on," said Gaurav.

"That woman was—?" Siddique asked doubtfully.

"Soren's wife. Baaji did the work on the streets then unlike the recent past when Gabbar handled it. Soren always accompanied Baaji. The gangs always have tension between them and so, they have spies in the other gang. Soren got paid by Akhtar to finish Baaji. He was almost successful but he missed very narrowly.

"That scar near the eye that Baaji has is due to that attempt. There was no escaping from that. Soren was killed brutally and his body was displayed outside Akhtar's house. This is still rumoured to be Gabbar's first kill. He had spotted Soren making a move and pushed him at the last minute.

"Baaji wanted revenge and Soren's life was not

enough. The gangs were in the street and beating each other every day. The department arrested Gabbar and we were building a case but that infuriated Baaji further. To curb the violence, they brought me in. I organised peace talks and got Akhtar, Baaji and Rajan in a room.

"After a war of words, Baaji agreed to let it go on the condition that his son was released from the case. The DCP was there with me and he did not agree to that. The department could not afford to let Gabbar go. There was strong evidence against him and the murder was all over the news," said Gaurav.

"Gabbar has no cases against him as far as I know," said Siddique.

"He has no active cases. He was cleared in this murder by the courts," said Gaurav.

"How? The department had evidence," said Siddique.

"The witness backtracked," said Gaurav.

"Who was the witness?" Siddique asked.

"Soren's wife," said Gaurav.

"She went against her husband?" Siddique asked, looking surprised.

"She had no choice. They killed her younger son and threatened to do the same with the other boy," said Gaurav gravely.

"I never knew this," said Siddique.

"You were not meant to. I negotiated that. I am not proud of this but I could not let them kill the woman and her son. Baaji agreed to give them five lakh rupees for their silence. Soren's wife was placed in the protection of Akhtar and the gangs were to end the fighting immediately. Gabbar was a free man. Akhtar was fine having peace again and the woman and her son could keep their lives," said Gaurav.

"Why did you question her?" Siddique asked.

"The boy was seventeen when this happened. He was brought up by a gangster. Revenge is in his blood. He wanted it then and he could still want it. It is not easy to let go of someone who killed your own blood, no matter how strong they are," said Gaurav.

"Do you think it is him?" Siddique asked.

"I will check with his workplace. I spoke to the boy and kept tabs on him for the first year. The woman did a good job of diverting him from the life his father lived but I have to check this anyway," said Gaurav.

"Do you want me to check?" Siddique asked.

"I have heard that you are trustworthy but let me do this," said Gaurav dismissively.

***

4:30 PM

"Hey Gaurav. What do we have so far?" the DCP asked, peeping from the door as Gaurav looked through the photos with Siddique.

"So far? Nothing," said Gaurav seriously.

"Not nothing," said Siddique reluctantly.

"Well, Mr Siddique here seems to think that a ghost could have killed Gabbar," said Gaurav with a wry grin.

"Be serious, guys! I am getting an earful each time I meet a superior officer. You have no idea how bad those conversations are. I have to hide under my desk to avoid being abused," said the DCP sternly.

"I am looking at it but I have nothing to work with," said Gaurav.

"Forget finding the killer. You are here to contain the situation," said the DCP as he was leaving the room.

"What does he mean? I thought they were joking when they said that you were not here to solve the case," said Siddique in a hushed voice.

"You know nothing about me, do you?" Gaurav asked.

"I don't know much but I hear that the senior officers like you very much. They say that your work is brilliant and you have clean hands," said Siddique.

"Oh. That is good to hear. I am the guy they call to settle disputes. I make sure fights stop by negotiating with criminals. Remember Soren? My work usually ensures that clashes are suppressed with talks. The public should not be endangered by these clashes. That is where I come in," said Gaurav.

"At least you protect the public," said Siddique appreciatively.

"Let's see," said Gaurav, looking at the evidence.

He had come to the department with lots of hopes and dreams. It took him a long while to find ways to actually do some good and it was nothing like what he had expected it to be. In this case, he had no idea what he was doing.

He was desperate to do something good but he knew that there was little that he could do. He dialled his wife's number to talk to his family. He chatted with them for a long time as Krishna drove him home.

***

6:15 PM

Akhtar had three wives and five children. His family was very close and his wives did not differentiate among their children. The eldest, Ajmal, was the heir to the business. Ajmal had intentions to make his father's business bigger. Deep down, he was as ruthless as his father, but he maintained a clean image.

Ajmal had a sister and three half-brothers, one of whom had gone abroad for studies. Akhtar's younger son was studying in a prestigious school in the city. Ajmal cared for him more than his other siblings and wanted them to stay away from the business. He ensured they were insulated from it.

He had big plans but it wasn't completely endorsed by his father yet. His father kept telling him not to be greedy. He kept insisting that they should be content with what they have. Akhtar was more interested in helping his people than expanding his business. He set up an agency that sent people to work as contract labour in the Middle East.

Ajmal spent most of his time at the office. He knew everything there was to know about the business. It kept him busy but it did not keep him happy. He continued to do it out of respect for his father. He ventured into a lot of other activities but he always sought his father's opinion. It was more out of respect than faith in his decisions.

Akhtar was growing old but he still had an aura about him. He could still roam about the city alone without any protection and nobody would dare to even look at him the wrong way. His first wife never left the house. She was the one who cooked for all members of the gang.

Every member of his inner circle ate at his house at least once a day. Akhtar's second wife, Shaheena, was a strong woman. Rumour was that she backed Ajmal to take over after her husband. Ajmal treated her with respect, just like his own mother. Shaheena was an excellent strategist and even people outside their gang knew about her.

Her ideas were more suited for Ajmal's sophisticated approaches. She was aggressive and shared her husband's lust for blood. She was involved in most of the important decisions in the gang. Akhtar knew of this but he did not disapprove it. He had married a woman less than half his age a few years ago. She was his third wife.

Many speculated that he did it just to make a point—that he was not getting old. The woman had given birth to a child not too long ago. His fifth child was younger than his grandson via Ajmal.

The word on the street was that Ajmal had tensions with Baaji in particular. Not too long ago during a mediation, Baaji had slapped him in front of his own men. He wasn't in a business where he could afford to lose face. There was a lot of animosity between them. There had been frequent fights, destruction of property and tipping the police to obstruct business.

It seldom escalated beyond that. It was a different story with his father. Akhtar had never forgiven his sister for marrying his enemy. He had no love left for her. He had claimed many times that he wanted everyone in Rajan's family dead including his sister and her children.

There was a rumour that he would give a generous reward to anyone who could do the deed. Both the father and son were capable of planning a hit on Gabbar but these were men who liked to claim credit. While they would not admit it publicly, their men would be aware and they would ensure that the rivals were notified. It was their vanity. Gabbar would have been their most important kill. Proving it would be difficult but it would be an open secret.

Ajmal stood with a few of his trusted men, talking about Gabbar's murder. "What is the word on the street? How is Rajan reacting to this?" he asked his men.

"Nobody has come out of the house so far. Rajan is on his terrace and he hasn't slept since they got the news. They are still waiting for the body. Things are calm," said one of his men confidently.

"This is the calm before the storm. Keep watching them. We are not going to make any moves. Am I clear?" Ajmal said, looking around. He saw each of his men nod at him. He waited to make sure that he was satisfied that they were clear and then dispersed them.

His father was nearby, sitting with his oldest wife. They were watching a show on the television but his attention was focused on his son. Akhtar knew that his son wanted to be his successor. He had been monitoring him for the past few months. He had changed a lot from when he first joined the business.

He was calmer, more likeable and smarter. He only needed a bit of patience to become complete. Akhtar was not too keen on handing over but it seemed right to do it early. Very few people got the opportunity to get out when they were on top.

He sat on his armchair, thinking about Ajmal. His wife was sitting on the floor, next to him. He had asked her to massage his legs but she was engrossed in the show. He had one thing left to do before he handed everything over to Ajmal. He had to do something about Rajan, Nasreen and the children they had together.

That was something that he had not handled. He did not want to pass that on to Ajmal. Ajmal did not feel the same way about the marriage. Even after so many years, Akhtar could not forgive his sister. He had loved her more than anyone else in the world. He had practically raised her and she had betrayed him for his enemy.

He would not have agreed even if she had asked him for permission. Aside from being from a different religion, Rajan was not an honourable man. Honour mattered most in his profession.

"We have been putting off Hajj for a long time now," said Akhtar as he gently placed his hands on his wife's shoulder. Akhtar was religious and he considered the Hajj as a mandatory duty. He had gone once with his grandmother. He did not have the means then but he had made it work.

His grandmother had raised him and he felt that it was a small way to repay her for her kindness. He had not gone since then. Looking at his wife, he felt that this was something she was owed.

"We could go but you have your work," said the woman.

"It is cute that you call it work after all these years," said Akhtar with a smile.

"I don't care what the rest of the people say. There

is no better man than you," she said, placing her arm on his knees and leaning on the handle of his chair. He suspected Ajmal's involvement in Gabbar's murder but he decided not to ask him about it.

"I am thinking of giving it all to Ajmal very soon. I think I am still able. You and I could go. If the other two want to join, they can too. We could go and leave all this behind for a few weeks," he said.

"I would like that," said the old woman, looking very pleased.

"I just have one small thing to complete. Let me finish that and I can retire. I will spend the rest of my life with my women," said Akhtar.

"You never know. This could be more fun than whatever you have been doing," she said as she stood up on her feet.

"We will have to see if that is the case," said Akhtar. He sat looking at Ajmal as his wife walked away. He meant what he said. He had lived an eventful life. He had done everything he wanted to do. He had been respected and feared. There was only one regret in his life. Rajan lived with his sister and he could not stand that.

He knew that Baaji was distracted now. If Ajmal had killed Gabbar to settle his score with Baaji, a long war was inevitable. He believed that Ajmal was smart enough to cover his tracks. If that was the case, things would go a lot smoother. Whether Ajmal had done this or not, this was an opportunity.

Rajan was the weakest he had been in years and this was an opportunity. Perhaps this was god's way of letting him know. He was going to finish them off once and for all. Once he had closure in this matter, he would be at peace.

CHAPTER 5

CLAIMING CREDIT

A FEW WEEKS AGO

"Are you insane?" Dr Niranjana asked in a loud voice. She looked around and noticed that everyone was looking at them. She looked apologetic and pulled Angel into one of the nearby rooms.

"I don't know what else to do," said Angel with tears.

"This is not just about aborting the foetus. This will harm your health. You may never be able to have children again," said the doctor, trying to sound kind.

"Maybe that is for the best," said Angel sadly.

"Let me talk to your husband," said Dr Niranjana, looking concerned. The man who had come with her stood in the corridor, watching a video on his phone. She moved towards him. "Don't worry. I know how to handle these conversations."

"I have no husband and that is my brother," said Angel, holding the doctor's hand. The look on the doctor's face was humiliating. The doctor held both her hands and looked at her with genuine concern. "It is not what you think. The child is not my brother's. He wouldn't do that," she told the doctor reassuringly. *He would do everything else,* she thought sadly.

"If you need help," began the doctor doubtfully. There was a look of pity in her eyes and Angel was glad about that look. Nobody took pity on her. Not her brother or the man who had made her pregnant. It did not lift her spirit but it was better than nothing.

"Tell her brother that she will die if she undergoes an abortion," said a voice that gave both women a scare. A male nurse sat in the corner with his lunch and spoke casually.

"What if—?" Dr Niranjana began.

"She is worth more to him alive. The more important question is whether you want to have this baby," said the male nurse, looking straight at Angel.

Angel looked at the man and nodded. He made sense. He was right. She was her brother's golden goose. Despite her circumstances, having the power to make this choice felt good.

"Do you want me to tell him now?" Dr Niranjana asked hopefully.

"He doesn't know yet. It can wait," said Angel politely. She turned to the male nurse and nodded politely. She turned and walked out of the room in better spirits.

Nawaz looked at the woman as she walked away.

She did not know who he was but he knew all that he needed to know about her. He did not know if it would be useful but he felt like this was a sign.

***

8:30 PM (PRESENT DAY)

In another part of the city, Cyrus was sitting in his room, deep in thought. He had heard about the murder and he was indifferent. He did not care about Gabbar but he was evaluating the implications his murder would have for him. "Any word on who killed Baaji's son?" Cyrus asked his most trusted man, Isaac.

"No. The police are all over the area but there has been no news about all this," said Isaac sincerely.

"I don't think Baaji wants the police to find the killer. You know him. Any word on the street?" Cyrus asked.

"It is surprisingly quiet. I want to know myself. It takes a lot of guts to even think of attacking them. Doing it," said Isaac, looking impressed.

"Anything from Akhtar's gang?" Cyrus asked.

"No. I don't think they did it. Akhtar and Ajmal love to take credit even if they arrange for other people to take the fall," said Isaac.

"The police should be restless," said Cyrus.

"They have got some DSP named Gaurav involved especially for this. He used to be quite the star," said Isaac.

"I remember the name. I don't seem to be able to put a face to the name. Is he any good?" Cyrus asked.

"He is but not in the way you think," said Isaac.

"What do you mean?" Cyrus asked, looking confused.

"If they got this guy in, they are not concerned about finding the killer. They are working towards a compromise," said Isaac.

"How is that even possible?" Cyrus asked with a grin. Baaji's son was dead. There would be blood, lots of it. Nothing was going to stop Baaji from seeking vengeance.

"I know but this guy used to be quite good at this. He was the one who settled our mall issue," said Isaac, recounting a sensitive negotiation years ago.

"I wondered why I knew the name. He was good but there is nothing in this world that can cool Baaji down. Especially when his son has been murdered so publicly. I expect Rajan to react at the earliest. It is not like him to be silent. Rajan loved Gabbar like his own son," said Cyrus.

"It does not matter. This is not about whether he loved Gabbar or not. This is about his reputation. His own blood was killed. Rajan will not take it lightly," said Isaac.

"So, the police are looking to mediate here. They want no violence," said Cyrus.

"That is how it looks. Rajan will have a lot of pull

but the police will be pressured to protect the city," said Isaac thoughtfully.

"What do you think we should do?" Cyrus asked.

"Take the blame," said Isaac immediately.

"Baaji and Rajan will come after us with everything they have. We cannot handle a gang war," said Cyrus.

"That is the best part. We will be protected by the police," said Isaac.

"Rajan has enough police in his pocket. We will simply be taking unnecessary attention," said Cyrus dismissively.

"This is a matter of serious law and order and the press will be vigilant too. The police will do their job," said Isaac. "If you want, I will set it up in my name. The word on the street will be that they did it under my command without your knowledge. That way you will be protected."

"They won't believe it. If they do, I will look weak," said Cyrus.

"You came into this life because your father was killed. Years later, you are no closer to avenging his death," said Isaac.

"We don't know if Baaji or Rajan killed him. It could have been anyone else. Even Akhtar is a possibility," said Cyrus doubtfully.

"Akhtar usually takes credit but he is not smart enough for a clean crime in such a high-profile murder. His vanity is his weakness. Trust me," said Isaac.

"That is true but this is a different story. Gabbar is important but not like my father. There are personal issues between them. Akhtar would probably gloat if he murdered Gabbar but I hear he has been very silent. The police are clueless too, you say," he told Isaac, looking at him doubtfully.

"It has only been two days but that is still a long time. Whoever did this wants to stay hidden. Let us make the most of it. We can take the blame. I can get a couple of people to surrender for the crime. I will spread the word that it was me who paid them. You will be shielded but people will know to give you credit," said Isaac.

"I will lose face. It will look like you are undermining me," said Cyrus.

"This isn't some upstart. This is Gabbar. Think about it. Everyone knows where my loyalties lie. They will know where to look if my name pops up. I am keeping you insulated from the legal proceedings. There won't be any doubt in the underground," said Isaac.

Cyrus sat in thought. If it were someone else, he could have suspected an ulterior motive but Isaac was loyal to a fault. He knew his place and he loved it there. He had treated Cyrus like a son all along though Cyrus did not feel the same way. There was always a risk in his business and sooner or later, he had to face the other two dons.

He could never forget his father's murder. The police could never find the killer and nobody claimed credit. That was for a reason. This murder was too high-profile to claim. One of the two dons had murdered his father. Neither of them had taken credit but Cyrus had enough reason to believe that it was one of them.

He always wanted to take both of them out for what happened to his father. This seemed like a good opportunity. It would make him a target but that did not matter. If he could not find who killed his father, he would finish both the dons just to be sure. This was something he should have done long ago. He had been doubting whether he was strong for too long. This was too good an opportunity to miss.

***

11:43 PM

Gaurav woke up to the sound of his phone ringing. He looked out and it was still dark. He looked at the clock and it was almost midnight. There were fifteen missed calls. He saw the name SI Siddique on the screen as he quickly dialled his number.

"What is it, Siddique?" Gaurav asked. He desperately wanted to catch up on some sleep but this was important.

"I just got a call from the station. There is another body in the marina," said Siddique.

"I will be there in twenty minutes," said Gaurav. He saw no need to call Krishna at this hour. It was late and she had a long day just like him.

Gaurav reached the marina in twenty minutes. There were four policemen standing at the beach and they were marking the crime scene as he entered it. Unlike Gabbar's murder scene, there were no people standing around the area. A man's body had been washed ashore and reported by the locals.

Just like Gabbar, the body was badly bruised and cut in several places. It seemed like the man was beaten badly and thrown into the sea with something heavy tied to his feet. The ropes on his feet looked damaged, possibly by the fishes or rocks on the ocean floor. Whoever had killed him had intended for the body to never be found.

However, the police had the body now and there was a possibility that they would find evidence on it. He yawned widely and stretched to get focused. Instinct told Gaurav that this had been done by the same person or gang that had taken out Gabbar. Unlike the previous crime scene, they had not wanted the body to be found. That alone felt like a breakthrough.

Gaurav knew that if he acted fast, he could find out who was behind this. There were not many people who could do such violent crimes within the marina area. This was the second killing in Baaji's territory. A handful of his gang members were watching the scene from a distance.

"Do we have a name?" Gaurav asked a constable as he walked to the scene. He surveyed the scene while looking at the gang members who were watching them. He wanted to check if anyone looked suspicious. Nobody seemed out of the ordinary.

"Not yet. The SI said he knew him. He is talking to some people over there," said one of the men marking the area with tape.

Gaurav walked further to see Siddique talking to a burly looking fellow near the body. The man looked uneasy to be there. Seeing Gaurav, Siddique tried awkwardly to salute but his arm in a sling did him no favours. Gaurav did not care. He waited for Siddique to finish his conversation. That was more important than a salute.

"Two bodies in the marina?" Gaurav asked as Siddique finally finished his conversation.

"It isn't the bodies that surprise me. It is finding them. People go missing all the time here. We never manage to find them," said Siddique calmly.

"Looks like bad luck. The rope was old and didn't hold the body to whatever it was tied to," said Gaurav, looking closely at the body. The body was bloated having been underwater.

"I have asked the coroner to confirm the time of death. Will this be related to Gabbar's murder?" Siddique asked.

"I think so. They both look to have been beaten

to death in a similar manner but the wounds look very different. I can't say anything yet but it does look like it now. Until it is proved otherwise, I will proceed assuming that both killers are the same," said Gaurav, looking at the wounds.

"This guy, Blade, was supposed to have been in his native village, which is a few hours away. He left four days ago and was not expected for a week," said Siddique.

"Blade?" Gaurav asked.

"That's what they called him. He was always around Gabbar. He was one of his closest people," said Siddique.

Feroz was at the site and he looked annoyed. He nodded at Gaurav as he came to him. Something peculiar had struck Gaurav in both crime scenes. He waited for Feroz to come to him and took him out of earshot. He hesitated and then called Siddique to accompany them.

"You saw the body?" he asked Feroz.

"Brutal," said Feroz, shaking his head.

"Are you thinking about a personal angle here?" Gaurav asked.

"You cannot rule out a crime of passion but this is a gang murder. Often, they both go hand-in-hand," said Feroz.

"A gang murder is one thing. Gabbar's body was displayed but they took the pain to try to hide this body," said Gaurav.

"If Gabbar was the target, I would not want to spook him. That is why they hid the first body and then displayed Gabbar," said Feroz.

"This seems personal too. If they want to take him out and hide him, why did they have to be so brutal? This seems very personal," said Gaurav as he eyed the body.

"How do you say that?" Siddique asked.

"Whoever did this had taken their time. They wanted to cause much pain. We still have not got the report but I see far too many injuries than required here and there is more than one type of injury. We are missing something. We need to check who had a reason for vengeance against Gabbar," said Gaurav.

"Vengeance against Gabbar? That will be a big list. I will look into this angle but I am not sure what I can get you on this body. It has been underwater for a few days and I don't think we will have any viable evidence," said Feroz.

Feroz left them but Siddique kept looking at Gaurav with a confused expression on his face. "You think this was vengeance?" he asked Gaurav.

"Looks like it. I have seen plenty of kills in my life. This doesn't look like a gang murder. Whoever did this had been keeping an eye on this area for a while. They must have known where each person would have been. Without that, they could not have done these murders," said Gaurav.

"That is impossible. We may not have this area under surveillance but Rajan does. Nothing happens here without his knowledge," said Siddique.

"I know Rajan's power in this area but Rajan relies on people. It is not like he has cameras around here. People have limitations and there is a way to outwit any person. I am just not able to figure out how it could have been done. I need to think like the killer to see how this could have been done," said Gaurav.

"You think it could have been Bhadra?" Siddique asked.

"Don't be stupid. You are a policeman. Don't tell me that you really believe in ghosts," said Gaurav dismissively.

"I don't know. I have been in this area all my life and Bhadra has been here all along. Several people have seen Bhadra. It could be true. There are things beyond our comprehension," said Siddique.

"This isn't one of those, trust me. Bhadra had nothing to do with this. Bhadra is a fabricated story built over the years to keep this area secluded, so that they can carry out their illegal activities. There are no ghosts in the real world," said Gaurav.

"I don't know. I don't believe in ghosts either but Bhadra—" began Siddique nervously.

"Something is wrong here. We need more information. I am moving ahead with the assumption that this was done by another human. Go to the forensics team and request them to prioritise this job and go home. Until we get more information, we will be chasing ghosts in this case. The forensic reports will shed more light on this case. Nevertheless, we need to go hunting for information tomorrow," said Gaurav.

"Where?" Siddique asked.

"You'll see," said Gaurav.

***

10:30 AM

Gaurav slept in the station that night to avoid wasting time driving home. He spent most of the early morning reaching out to his old contacts. He still remembered most of their phone numbers. Many could not believe that he was really calling them. While most of them were not important, one particular person was crucial. This person did not have the habit of using phones.

"We need to go to Mehbooba market immediately," said Gaurav.

"Why?" Siddique asked, getting into the jeep.

"We need to meet Gun Baba," said Gaurav quickly.

"Why him? He doesn't belong to any gang," said Siddique.

"I'm surprised you are working in this area and don't know why," said Gaurav.

Gun Baba was a well-known name in the underworld but most people had never met him. His real name was Gunshev Popov. He claimed to be of both Bulgarian and Russian descent but nobody knew much about him other than his trade. He had come to the city during the collapse of the USSR and stayed here since then.

He had monopoly over the guns in the city. At times, he ventured into designer drugs and foreign flesh trade, which he sold directly to the dons and politicians. He was more powerful than the police, dons and politicians. Most importantly, he was on excellent terms with everyone. There wasn't anything that happened in the city that he didn't know about.

He was known to be discreet with his information but he helped the police solve difficult cases without hurting his business or reputation. He preferred the city being peaceful too. He claimed that it was better for business.

Most people couldn't pronounce his name. Over time, Gunshev Popov had become Gun Baba. Gaurav had met him twice before this. Once, when he had to find a group who had kidnapped a central minister's daughter, and the other time, when he wanted to find a stolen weapon of one of his superiors.

The first time, it had been a friendly chat where Gun Baba was eager to help. He had given Gaurav useful information using which, a task-force had rescued the girl before any serious harm was done. The second time, he had been reluctant. He did not care about the gun or the official who had lost it.

As a last resort, Gaurav had to strong arm him into giving him the info. He knew that this would destroy their relationship but it was essential at that time and he knew that he would soon be transferred out of that department. Gaurav recognised the familiar location as the jeep came to a halt.

Gun Baba stayed in Mehbooba market. While he owned a store, nobody was sure what exactly was sold there. He sold a lot of items every now and then. While the other shopkeepers in the market had loyalties towards one of the dons in the city, they were on good terms with him. Nobody would ever give him up to the police.

Gun Baba did not look like a foreigner. He was a tall man with a tan that made him look like a native. His attire defined him as well. He seemed more like a poor shopkeeper rather than a notorious dealer. He hadn't changed one bit since Gaurav had last seen him. His brown hair had always had streaks of grey. It was levelled but untidy. He was scratching his hair as Gaurav walked up to his store. He did not look happy seeing Gaurav but he gestured him to step into the back of the shop. The man was selling cooking oil now.

The door to the back of the shop gave them a surprise. It seemed like a whole different world on the other side. The place was spotless and tiled brightly. There was a plush sofa, a teapoy and two ordinary chairs. Gaurav knew why the chairs were ordinary. Gun

Baba liked to show people their place.

Gaurav sat in one of the ordinary chairs and asked Siddique to sit in the other. Gun Baba took almost fifteen minutes to come and settled himself comfortably on the sofa. As though on cue, a scantily clad woman came with three tall glasses of juice.

In another life, this woman could have been in a Hollywood movie. She had an expressionless face as she served the juice. She then sat on the sofa. Gun Baba casually placed his feet on her lap. She began to massage it without minding them.

Gaurav eyed Siddique, who looked angry seeing the behaviour. The man looked at his superior and controlled his emotions. They were here for information.

"How can I help?" he asked politely.

"I will get straight to it. Do you know anything about Gabbar's murder?" Gaurav asked sharply.

The grin vanished from Gun Baba's face. "Go away," he said curtly to the woman. Once she was out of earshot, he turned to Gaurav. He narrowed his eyes and looked at Gaurav. He flexed his shoulders and leaned forward. "I don't like insinuations. I had nothing to do with it," he said quickly.

"I know you had nothing to do with it. You would have done it much differently. Besides, you don't need to. I would suspect my colleague here before I suspect you," said Gaurav as he relaxed on his chair.

Gun Baba smiled. He looked at Siddique and

widened his smile. "He looks innocent," joked the tall Russian. "If I am not a suspect, why are you here?" he asked politely. His grin returned to his face.

"I need your help. This will become a war if we don't find something," said Gaurav.

"It will become a war even if you find something. In fact, it already is a war. This is Rajan's own blood," said Gun Baba.

"You can help me stop it from becoming worse. You can help me minimise violence," said Gaurav in a low voice. He deliberately wanted to look weak in the conversation. The last time they had met, he had strong armed the man. This time, he wanted to handle this smoothly. The sooner he got the information, the better.

"Why do you think I would know something? Even if I did, what would I gain from talking to you?" Gun Baba asked.

"Nothing happens in this city without your knowledge. At least, not something of this magnitude. I don't know about gain but a gang war will affect your business. You can keep selling weapons but all your other businesses will take a hit. Not to mention more attention from police," said Gaurav pointedly.

Gun Baba looked at Gaurav for a moment. His eyes then moved to each policeman for a while. He looked like he was evaluating what was the best scenario. "I have nothing concrete," he said slowly.

"Anything from you will help. I have nothing, concrete or otherwise," said Gaurav.

"So far, the gangs are all silent. This is something people will want to claim credit for. Cyrus is talking but I don't believe him," said Gun Baba.

"Why not? He has had his differences with both the gangs," said Gaurav.

"He has the balls but not the brain for something like this. This doesn't look like an execution and I saw the photos. It wasn't clean," said Gun Baba.

"How did you get the photos?" Siddique asked anxiously. Both men ignored him.

"Cyrus wants to take credit but you think he did not do it?" Gaurav asked.

"I am certain. Trust me, I hear things like this before it happens. There have been people trying to put a hit on Gabbar but nothing went through. There are people who can do things without my knowledge and Cyrus is not one of them," said Gun Baba.

"Hits? How do you know?" Siddique asked doubtfully.

"I know and that is none of your business. I am talking to your boss here," said Gun Baba rudely.

"Anything else?" Gaurav asked, gesturing Siddique to keep quiet.

"Believe me, I would prefer to end this war before it starts too," said Gun Baba.

"Keep me informed on anything you hear. I will

keep visiting on a daily basis until this is over," said Gaurav.

"I have your number. I will keep my eyes and ears open. I know how to reach you. I will keep you updated frequently but don't visit me again for this. I hope you understand," said Gun Baba.

Gaurav nodded and walked back to his car. As they walked back to the car, Siddique looked surprised. "He was very cooperative," he said.

"Not by choice," said Gaurav gravely. Gunshev Popov knew the damage his business would take due to a war. He knew that the war had to be stopped by any means possible. Even if it meant letting go of his ego to save his business. If he was doing this with minimal persuasion, the situation was worse than Gaurav thought.

CHAPTER 6

NEGOTIATING WITH POWERHOUSES

Gaurav had expected the gangs to be calm until Gabbar's funeral. There were rituals that lasted for ten days and Baaji would not step out till then. The violence was expected to be minimal but they were wrong. While Baaji and Rajan were at home in mourning, the gang members were getting out of control. They were on the streets already, picking fights. The gangs had maintained a balance, having restricted themselves to specific areas in the past, but all that was forgotten now.

In the first two days since Gabbar had died, thirteen murders took place in the city. One man from Rajan's gang and twelve from the other gangs had been killed. There had been more than two dozen clashes in the streets and the police were doing their best to keep the violence to a minimum.

The dons were looking for an opportunity to showcase their power and the wannabes were eager to prove their mettle to their bosses. There was also the breaking down of shops, burning of vehicles and every other atrocity that one associated with the death of someone influential. There were far too many cases for the existing police force to handle.

The IG had brought in additional police force from other parts of the state. She had doubled the city-wide patrols, tripled it in sensitive areas and violence was still not under control. When everyone in an area was out to damage anything in sight, even the police were helpless.

The IG wanted a lockdown in sensitive areas but with the elections less than a year away, the chief minister denied her request. He also denied requests for using tear gas and other riot control measures.

***

9:30 AM

Gaurav sat in the meeting room that had been allocated to him temporarily. He was thinking while running his fingers over his moustache. He was watching the news and there was violence in every part of the city. Time was running out and everyone in the department was under pressure. He knew that there was only one course of action now but the DCP would not like it.

"You can't be serious. I am no politician, Gaurav! I do not have that kind of pull," shouted DCP Patel.

"You said the higher ups told you that they will help you with anything," said Gaurav.

"Those people asking us to help are like unfriendly

relatives asking you if you had food. You nod, smile and walk away. You don't take them up on their offer," said the DCP.

"You want me to do the impossible. The department wants you to oversee that. This is the only way to do it," said Gaurav. He waited for a moment and then added softly, "I have thought this through. There is no other way."

Rajan was not going to sit for a negotiation in this matter. Definitely not when his own brother's only son had been murdered. He would lose face and also have to deal with his brother. Gabbar was everything to Baaji. They still had no idea who the murderer was and Rajan had political clout.

The law minister, Sharad Thakur, was the only person Rajan would listen to. He was the person who had made Rajan who he was and he commanded Rajan's loyalty. He was the person who had tasked the DCP to contain the situation. Even if the minister did not like this, he would have to do it to ensure that he retained his ministry.

The whole state was watching this via the media who were closely monitoring everything. Rajan would not back down for anyone else. The department usually avoided placing such requests to politicians but this was unavoidable. Gaurav had thought this through. This had to be done fast. Once Gabbar's funeral was over, there would be a bloodbath.

"Come with me. Let us go meet him," said the DCP abruptly.

"Come with you? I don't want to meet him," said Gaurav immediately.

"I shouldn't be the only one facing the music, should I? Drop everything. Let us go now," he said with a smirk.

The ride to the minister's office was a silent one. The DCP was not smirking anymore. He did not show it but Gaurav knew that he was running the conversation in his mind.

***

10:15 AM

"Patel, I did not expect to see you here. Did you find the killer?" the minister asked as he walked by them. He was a tall man and looked fit. He wore gold framed spectacles that made him look smart. He wore more gold than he needed. He was followed by a number of his lackeys but he invited the DCP into his office. The DCP pulled Gaurav by hand as he walked in. He was not going to do this alone.

"This is the guy you had me pull from the governor's office?" the minister asked as he showed them their seats. He looked at the DCP, who stared at him awkwardly. "If you have nothing, why come to see me?" the minister asked.

"We want your help," said Gaurav sharply.

"Help with what?" the minister asked, looking surprised. He did not expect the DSP to talk when his superior, the DCP, remained quiet.

"We want them to have a talk. We want to suppress this before there is violence," said the DCP awkwardly.

"There is violence already. I got you additional police force already. If you want something else, get to the point," said the minister, looking disinterested. He leaned back on his chair, lit a cigarette and looked directly at them.

"We want you to get Rajan to come for a meeting with the other bosses in the city. There is no way we can make him come," said the DCP reluctantly.

The minister swore loudly. "You want me to do your job for you? I don't want to call Rajan now," said the minister angrily.

"Sir, you don't want to but we can't. He will not listen to just another policeman. This isn't just about power. You are the only person he looks up to. You are the only one he will listen to. We are not coming to you because we want to take the easy way out. This is the only way to do this," said Gaurav softly.

The DCP realised that the expression on the minister's face had changed. He looked calmer than when Gaurav had begun speaking. A few minutes later, Gaurav walked with the DCP towards their car. The minister had agreed. The DCP had been silent the entire walk back to the car.

"I underestimated you," he said, breaking his silence.

"What?" Gaurav asked.

"It is not just the criminals you can negotiate with," said the man, smiling as he spoke.

"I did nothing," said Gaurav, trying hard not to smirk.

"You stroked his ego and got what we needed. I made a huge mistake by letting you go," said the man, punching Gaurav playfully. "Perhaps it was wise to let you go. If you had kept doing that, you might be my boss by now," said the man, looking impressed.

"Now I know that you are mocking me," said Gaurav as he reached for the door.

***

"What do we have on the second body?" Gaurav asked as he looked at the newspaper.

The media was keeping this on the down low. There were no exclusive coverages, no conspiracy theories and no allegations. The IG had organised a meeting to highlight the sensitivity of the issue to the media and they had agreed unanimously to give very little coverage to this news.

As Rajan had insisted, they had mentioned that Gabbar, an activist, had been ambushed and killed in the marina. There was no mention of the second body. Nobody cared about a random henchman. Siddique handed him the report for the second body.

"He died a couple of days before Gabbar," said Siddique, looking at the report over Gaurav's shoulder. "At least," he added quickly, looking at the details. There were five or six cuts on his body. He had been cut in his neck and thrown into the ocean. It was not clear where he had been dropped in the ocean or how. The rope that held him to the rock used for drowning him looked old. There was nothing useful in the report. He shook his head.

"That was around the time he went to his hometown. Someone who had intimate knowledge of this area is involved in this," said Gaurav thoughtfully. He was sure that this murder had something to do with Gabbar's murder. This could not be a coincidence. Someone had taken out Gabbar's aide. It almost seemed as though this murder was done to gain access to Gabbar. Or the murder was done by someone with access to Gabbar.

"A lot of people could have the motive but I doubt if anyone would have overcome their fear and gone through with it. Everyone knows how powerful this family is," said Siddique thoughtfully.

"Perhaps that is why they did it. Destabilising Rajan's family could be the motive," said Gaurav. Whoever it was, they had been watching Gabbar for a while. They knew enough to take out someone in his close circle and they had identified a perfect spot to kill him.

"It is possible but that is the stupidest motive I have heard of. Money does make people lose rationality," said Siddique sharply.

"Money and emotion," said Gaurav as he closed the report.

***

11:30 PM

"I want to know where they both are at all times," said Ajmal in a hoarse whisper. He looked to be tense as he held his phone. That was unlike him. "I know that he is dead but that does not change anything. I need you to do what you are doing and I need you to be more careful in doing that. You remember what happened to Soren, don't you? I want you to stay calm and do what you are doing," said Ajmal. He turned around and saw his father walking towards him. "I'll call you back," he said on the phone before ending the call.

"Who was that?" Akhtar asked calmly.

"Business," said Ajmal dismissively.

"Which business?" Akhtar asked sharply.

"You will get to know soon enough," said Ajmal and walked away.

Akhtar looked at his son and sighed. Ajmal was making many plans and he was holding back on them due to his respect for his father. Akhtar was either going to have to give his business to Ajmal or it was going to be grabbed from him. Ajmal was losing patience. Akhtar began to wonder if he was ready.

***

12:25 AM

The shopping complex had been closed around midnight. The DCP stood with Gaurav as they ate at a roadside shop overlooking the building. Fifteen policemen had been called in and they were all in mufti. This was going to be another long night. Krishna was waiting in the car within the complex and Siddique had been given the night off.

The meeting had been arranged by the law minister, Sharad Thakur. Nobody wanted to refuse a meeting with him. Everyone had confirmed attendance, including Rajan. Gaurav knew that this was big. Getting these people in a room alone would not have been enough. It would have been a brawl.

The presence of the minister in the meeting would change everything. Everyone would be on their best behaviour. The minister insisted on his own personal guard being there in the meeting. The other policemen were restricted to the streets. Only Gaurav and the DCP were to go in when the time came.

The minister was the first to arrive. He was casually

clothed. He wanted the people coming there to feel relaxed. The next person to arrive was Gun Baba. He came alone and walked in. Akhtar came next, accompanied by a few of his men and his son, Ajmal. He was closely followed by Cyrus, who came with his trusted lieutenant, Isaac.

Both men had more than a dozen men accompanying them but they were all quickly sent away. There was to be no violence that night. They were in the presence of a powerful politician. The intention was a truce. A war would make life difficult for everyone. Six other gangsters from the city had been invited but none of them were even remotely capable of something like this. All the focus was on Akhtar and Cyrus. The DCP and most people in the department were convinced that one of the two had done this.

Once everyone had gone into the building, Rajan was given the signal. He was to arrive from the other entrance. Gaurav did not want a confrontation until everyone was in the room. He had mediated small level murders, assaults and a few kidnaps. He had never mediated something of this level.

While it was something beyond what he had done, the rules of mediation were the same. They needed someone who was feared and respected by all to oversee the mediation. That was the law minister. They also needed a neutral location. The shopping complex was the perfect choice. The other requisite was containing the aggrieved.

As Rajan Bhai's vehicle approached, the DCP and Gaurav watched as most of the policemen converged towards their car. They did not want them to come with weapons. The DCP looked tense as he waited for communication on his wireless.

"Rajan Bhai and Baaji have reached. He is entering the complex. We have checked them for weapons," said a voice.

"That is our cue," said the DCP as he walked forward. "If it were not for you, I would be asleep at home," he muttered as they entered the complex.

"Wouldn't I love that too," said Gaurav as they walked in quickly. They wanted to reach the room before Rajan Bhai.

Rajan had come in street clothes. He looked calm but his usual grin was missing. Baaji looked angry and made no effort to hide it. Rajan walked in front of his brother, who scowled and frowned every step of the way. Baaji's anger overshadowed his grief.

Rajan nodded and bowed a little on seeing the minister and stared coldly at Akhtar and Ajmal as he took his seat. He turned to look at his brother. Baaji was staring at Cyrus and Akhtar, unsure of who he wanted to confront. He was looking for an answer.

"Why are we here, Mr Thakur?" Rajan asked politely. He paid no heed to the others. He wanted to let the others know that he was here only for the minister.

"Patience, Rajan. Take a seat. We are all here to talk," said the minister, pointing to the chair next to him. Rajan took the seat but Baaji was not interested in sitting and having conversations. He stood with a frown on his face. Rajan nudged his brother. Baaji was looking at both the other dons angrily.

"With all due respect, we are the only ones here who have lost family in the last week. I see no reason why we have to talk. Instead of questioning one of these cowards here, you bring us over to talk to them," said Baaji gruffly as he sat next to Rajan.

"Who are you calling a coward? If we lost someone, we would be on the streets and not looking to talk peace," said Isaac.

"I do not care where we are. I will rip your tongue out and feed it to you," said Baaji menacingly. Gaurav felt the chills when he spoke. This was a threat but made with perfection.

"Let us not start bickering amongst ourselves. We are here to talk," said Akhtar loudly. He raised his chest and made an effort to look taller than he already was.

"Easy for you to say. You did not lose someone in your family," said Baaji.

"You have my condolences, Baaji," said Akhtar.

"To hell with your condolences, old man," said Baaji as he rubbed his scar with his thumb. His eyes were fixed angrily on the older don.

Almost everyone stood up immediately and most

of them were ready to have a go at each other. Rajan was holding his brother back from jumping over the table and attacking Akhtar. The minister and the old don were the only ones who had not bothered to stand up. Akhtar looked at his fingers lazily and faked a yawn.

Baaji was jumping like he had springs under his feet and Rajan was struggling to hold him. In a few minutes, everyone settled down again. Rajan stared at Akhtar and everyone but Akhtar was looking at him.

The others were seated opposite to the minister and the brothers. Akhtar looked impassive while his son was holding back a laugh. He was delighted to see Baaji in discomfort. Most of the other gangsters were sitting nervously and just watching the big bad dons stare at each other. Cyrus looked amused on seeing Baaji but he remained silent. The minister was sitting quietly with his eyes closed.

"We know that you have suffered a great loss. We only want to clear the air so that nothing rash happens," said the DCP sharply.

"We have done nothing so far despite such an attack on us. Gabbar was like a son to me. Don't talk to me about clearing the air. I have asked my men to stand down but do not think that this is due to weakness. If I find which one of you is responsible for this, you will regret it," said Rajan calmly.

"Is that a threat?" Ajmal asked quickly. Akhtar kicked him from under the table but the boy had infuriated Baaji.

In a moment, Baaji was on his feet and was ready to throw his chair at Ajmal. For a man of his age with a paunch, he was surprisingly agile. He stepped on a chair and got on the table in a flash. Gaurav reached Baaji while his brother gripped his hand. Rajan struggled to hold his brother back but Baaji cooled down as soon as Rajan touched him.

"Stand down, Baaji. Rajan! Control your brother," said the minister sternly. Gaurav immediately understood why the minister was mediating the meeting. Everyone in the room was looking at him and even the grieving Baaji cowered. "Akhtar Bhai, I want a conversation that gives a solution. I don't want any wise cracks or taunts. Most of these kids are immature but I expected better of you," said the minister sharply.

"My son was a little overzealous, excuse him. That being said, we had nothing to do with this. If we did, we would have no problems accepting it. I have no reason to fear anyone in this city," said Akhtar calmly. He didn't even bother to look at the minister as he spoke. He was looking straight at Rajan as he spoke.

"If I wanted to take someone out in that pathetic excuse for a gang, I would take you out for having stolen my sister. I would have taken her out too for good measure," he said scathingly. Akhtar flexed his wrists and narrowed his eyes as he looked directly at Rajan.

"Firstly, you can't touch me. Secondly, your sister

loves me. I have treated her better than you ever could. She is my wife. You wanted to pimp her out," began Rajan hotly.

"One more word and I will end you on this spot. I loved my sister. You made her betray me," shouted Akhtar, looking furious.

"She is happier with me than she ever was with you," shouted Rajan.

"You defiled her with your—" said Akhtar, rising to his feet.

"Alright, settle down," said the minister, banging the table. He looked furious. He wanted to have a conversation and he was being disrespected. "I have had dealings with each one of you. Do not let that cloud your judgment. If you think you can make a war out of this, I will finish each and every one of you and your families. The city won't even remember you. If it is a choice between my position and you, I won't think twice before making a choice. Am I clear?" the minister asked looking around.

"I don't know which one of you was stupid enough to do this. If someone here had the guts to do this, you should have owned up to it. I don't see any of you doing that. I do not want violence on the streets. I do not want anything on the news. I definitely do not want the opposition using this to win the next election. I want you to sit here like men and discuss peace. Am I clear?" he asked again.

Every person in the room went silent the moment the minister had started speaking. Even Baaji did not talk back despite his obvious disappointment. Rajan looked surprised. He had expected the minister to support him but the minister was not choosing sides. He had made his intentions clear. Everyone else was staring at the minister.

"Gentlemen, let us get down to the matter at hand. We need peace now. We cannot have you people at each other's throats. That will affect the public," said the DCP. He stood erect and tried to make himself appear as tall and commanding as he could.

"We are not the ones who are looking to create violence. We have never been the ones to start a fight," said Cyrus dismissively.

"I lost a son. I did not start this fight. You will be fools if you think that I will not finish this fight," said Baaji hotly.

"Shut up, everyone. I will not sit by watching you people bicker in front of me. Rajan! I know your brother is grieving but I expect you to control him. His grief cannot be imagined but you understand how the world works," said the minister, rising to his feet.

"I know you have lost something, Baaji. I sympathise with you. No father should watch his son die. My condolences. That does not mean that we will let you start a war in the streets. I cannot let you do that. I am the law minister and I will be a laughing stock if I let it happen. We are here to negotiate a truce. Do not make the mistake of thinking that I am offering you a choice," said the minister sternly.

"It is not my son who died but Gabbar is as much a son to me as my own children," said Rajan. He was holding Baaji's hand as he spoke. Baaji was quiet and looking at his feet. "I understand that a war will hurt everyone. I don't agree but I understand. Give me the ones who killed him. Me and my brother will forgive the one who gave the order," said Rajan seriously. He looked directly at the minister and nodded pointedly.

"There cannot be more bloodshed. We have the press buzzing already," said Gaurav.

"I am giving you a way to avoid bloodshed. Give me the ones who killed him. I promise you won't even find the bodies," said Rajan curtly. Rajan had an ominous look on his face and glanced around the room. He looked everyone in the eye before finally looking at the minister. Gaurav looked at the minister in shock but the minister was calm. He looked like he was evaluating his options. After a full minute, he looked convinced.

"Fair enough. Can you do that? Give up your hitmen for peace? You won't get a better offer," said the minister.

Cyrus and Akhtar looked at each other as though they were expecting the other person to speak. Neither of them opened their mouths as Rajan and Baaji kept looking expectantly.

"You can reach my men anytime this week. Be ready to hand them over. You have my word that Rajan will not come after you if you do this," said the minister.

The other two dons left the room. Rajan waited until they were out of the room. "I am doing this for you, Thakur Saab. I will keep my men in order for now but the ones who killed Gabbar are mine. You give them to me and forget them," said Rajan sharply to the minister and walked away, followed by Baaji.

He turned to the DCP just before he exited the door. "Don't think about arrests or something smart. You do not want to mess this up for me. I have done a lot for you just by agreeing to this," said Rajan as he held his brother.

One by one, the dons left the building. Only the minister and the two policemen remained in the room. "That went well," said the minister, sitting down and stifling a yawn.

"We can't allow Rajan to take the men. He will kill them," said Gaurav, trying to appeal to the minister.

"The alternative is a war. Nobody wants that. Rajan is emotional. His pride is hurt," said the minister.

"We have to look the other way when he kills people?" Gaurav asked hotly.

"Wake up, Gaurav! Every person who was in this room is a killer. They have killed more people than we can count. We have to avoid violence on the street," said the DCP.

"We have to stroke his ego?" Gaurav asked, looking dismayed.

"For the greater good," said the DCP.

"You might want to get this sorted soon," came a voice from the table. They were surprised to see Gun Baba still seated in his chair in a corner, looking at them lazily. "I don't have a word on the killer yet but I hear that Isaac is looking to claim credit. That will get him a lot of attention," he said calmly.

"Why would he do that? He must have done it then," said the minister.

"Isaac talks the big talk but he cannot do something like this. He only wants to claim credit," said Gun Baba.

"That is stupid. Baaji will slaughter him. He must have a death wish," said Gaurav.

"Cyrus has been trying for years to find out who killed his father. We still don't know who did it, though I suspect both Rajan and Akhtar. Claiming credit will raise Cyrus' profile to a whole new level," said Gun Baba.

"That is stupid," said the DCP.

"I agree," said Gun Baba.

"Get a hold of this until we get a few names. Make sure Cyrus does not step out of the market. He is safe as long as he is there. If he is being as stupid as this, he is going to get himself killed," said the minister, walking out. The DCP followed him while discussing details.

Gaurav settled down next to Gun Baba and asked,

"Who do you think did it?"

"I told you. I am not sure. This could be like the death of Cyrus' father. We might never find an answer," said Gun Baba.

"Let me put it in a different way. Who could have done it? Who would have wanted to?" Gaurav asked.

"That's a good question," said Gun Baba with a chuckle. "That list would be endless. Gabbar had enemies everywhere, even inside his own gang. There have been too many calls to hitmen asking for Gabbar to be killed. A few were persistent. Any number of people could have killed him," said Gun Baba.

"Not everyone would have had the means to do it. Doing him in the marina would not have been easy for any commoner," said Gaurav.

"That is true. My best suspect inside their gang was found dead a few days after you found Gabbar," said Gun Baba.

"Who?" Gaurav asked.

"That friend of his. What's his name? Scissor or sharpener—" said Gun Baba, failing to recall the name.

"Blade?" Gaurav asked.

"Yes. He remained close to Gabbar but don't let that fool you. He had a good reason for wanting Gabbar dead," said Gun Baba.

"I don't follow," said Gaurav.

"Gabbar had an affair with this guy's sister. It is no secret that Gabbar has a weakness for women. Just looking into the families of these women who have been wronged by him should take a few weeks," said Gun Baba.

"I will look into this but the coroner puts the time of death of this guy two days before Gabbar. Would this guy be able to assemble a hit squad?" Gaurav asked.

"He could have got his hands on the cash. He has been Gabbar's blind spot for a while now. If he was killed, I doubt a hit squad would have followed through," said Gun Baba.

"Back to square one. Anyone else?" Gaurav asked.

"Do I get paid? I am practically doing your job," said Gun Baba.

"I am not arresting you. Deal?" Gaurav asked.

"That is the shittiest deal I have ever heard," said Gun Baba sarcastically.

"The sooner you help me close this, the sooner I disappear from your life," said Gaurav.

"You should have begun with that," said Gun Baba. "Six months ago, Gabbar kidnapped the son of an industrialist. I don't remember names. I only remember that he owns a steel factory near the highway."

"Baldev Singh, I know him. What exactly happened?" Gaurav asked.

"The negotiation didn't go well. This guy is a big shot and despite his best efforts, Gabbar kept the boy for four days, starving him before returning him home. Rajan was out of town but intervened immediately on his return. The boy suffered minimal physical damage but too much trauma. After a lot of efforts, Rajan brokered peace between all parties. Rajan lost it with Gabbar after that. He hadn't spoken to him ever since. I wouldn't put it past Rajan to sign off on this hit. That incident cost him a posting in the constituency," said Gun Baba.

"He would kill Gabbar for that?" Gaurav asked. "Forget I asked. He would kill for less," he added quickly.

"Everyone wanted Gabbar killed. It would be hard to find someone who did not want him dead. Even thinking about people with means would be a long list," said Gun Baba.

"So, we are back to square one," said Gaurav.

"You never left it. Your DCP and the minister want to stop a war. You can reason with Rajan but Baaji is blinded by rage. You can't stop this war unless you put Baaji in a cell. Unfortunately for you, he is the only one in this entire city I am sure did not kill Gabbar," said Gun Baba.

Gaurav looked at Gun Baba and realised the man was being honest. Nobody could stop Baaji from going on a rampage. He realised he would have to initiate another conversation with the DCP to ask the minister to speak to Rajan. That was not going to be pleasant.

***

6:30 PM

"Hello, Angel. I see that you are healthier than when I last saw you," said Dr Niranjana with a smile. The nurse from the other day was checking Angel's blood pressure.

"I have been taking care of myself," said Angel calmly.

"That is good. Have you told your brother?" Dr Niranjana asked.

"Not yet," said Angel immediately.

"We can try to get you help," began Dr Niranjana, looking concerned.

"Thank you but things have changed," said Angel sadly.

The doctor remained silent as she finished the procedure. Angel was placed on a wheelchair and guided outside by the nurse.

"You will have to tell your brother eventually," said the male nurse.

"I never heard your name," said Angel indifferently.

"I am Nawaz," said the man.

"It looks like I don't have to worry about telling him anymore. Nice to see you, Nawaz. I know it is your job but you are the first man to be nice to me without having the need to be," said Angel, getting off the wheelchair. She smiled weakly. Nawaz could see the sadness in her eyes. There was no masking that.

CHAPTER 7

LEADS AND DEAD ENDS

7:05 AM

Gaurav was being driven to the marina early in the morning. It was just after seven. Gaurav was half-asleep, reading the news on his mobile when he got a call from his wife. He picked up the call immediately.

"You are awake so early in the morning. Am I dreaming?" his wife asked.

"Miracles do happen," said Gaurav sarcastically.

"You didn't sleep all night, did you?" Sunitha asked, sounding concerned.

"Work is tight. You have been watching the news, haven't you?" Gaurav asked.

"I never watch the news. You tell me all that I need to know," she said.

"It is bad. You know Rajan Bhai, right? His brother's son was killed. That is why I had to cancel my holiday," said Gaurav.

"I can come. You are not sleeping. That means you definitely aren't eating properly. You won't take care of yourself," she said, sounding sincere.

"I will take care of myself, I promise. Stay there with the kids. You always take care of me. You deserve this time. This is a bad phase. This is like those days when I kept bad hours. Hopefully, I will be back to my regular job when you are back and we can slip back into our comfortable life," said Gaurav.

Sunitha began to talk about what the kids were doing. Gaurav had expected it to be a boring trip for the kids but it turned out to be good. The boys were being taught how to swim by their grandfather. She had also enrolled them in an online summer camp for kids. She was enjoying time with her mother and spending the evenings playing with the kids.

After hearing her out, he was sure this was a trip he would regret missing. He put the thought out of his mind and ended the call as he reached the spot where Siddique waited for him.

"Good morning," said Siddique as he got into the car.

"This won't be a good morning. The DCP bailed on us. We have to do this on our own," said Gaurav as Krishna drove the car towards their destination. They were going to the lion's den to have an uncomfortable conversation.

"I have never spoken directly to Rajan Bhai," said Siddique as they came to a halt.

"I know you haven't and this is definitely the worst

way to start a conversation with him," said Gaurav, washing his face to feel fresh.

"Do I have to come?" Siddique asked nervously.

"Of course you do. You don't expect me to face him alone, do you?" Gaurav asked.

"I still have to come back in the evening to live in this area," said Siddique quietly.

"We are only going to talk to him," said Gaurav but he understood what Siddique was thinking. Even policemen knew enough to fear Rajan. He was not a person who you wanted to cross paths with. If he wanted to hurt you, your position or power did not matter.

Rajan was seated in his balcony. The usually well-groomed don was looking dull in his unshaven look. He kept staring at the floor as they reached him. There was a cup of coffee next to him on his table, which looked like it had gone cold. Rajan was in a rare moment of weakness. He had been stronger on the day of Gabbar's death.

"Officers! I heard that you wanted to meet me," he said and called for his attendants. They quickly got a couple of chairs. He waited till all the attendants were gone. "Have you found who killed my boy?" Rajan asked in a low voice.

"We are investigating," said Gaurav quickly.

"You have nothing," said Rajan, leaning back on his chair.

"We are trying," said Gaurav defensively.

"Not hard enough. It has been days and you seem to have nothing for me," said Rajan.

"We are following a few promising leads," said Gaurav.

"I don't care what leads you have. If you find him, you bring him to me and not to your department. I will settle things with the minister," said Rajan.

"I have to run it by the DCP," said Gaurav slowly.

"Patel? Don't worry about him. I will make sure that the minister sends word to him," said Rajan assertively. He smiled confidently and looked like his image in the posters.

"This is not about that. We wanted to talk to you," said Gaurav.

"You wanted to talk to me? What for? Is someone interfering with your investigation?" Rajan asked, looking concerned.

Siddique began to scratch his head awkwardly. There was no easy way to do this. Gaurav looked at him and understood what he was thinking. "We would like to question you, if you don't mind," said Gaurav.

Rajan looked at them, confused. It hit him then. "You have got some nerve coming here to my house and telling me to my face that you think I killed him," said Rajan, his voice growing louder as he spoke each word.

"Mr Rajan, please," said Gaurav, trying to get him to calm down.

"Really? You want me to calm down? You accuse

me of killing my own blood and you want me to calm down?" Rajan asked, standing up and getting closer to Gaurav.

Siddique was nervous but Gaurav was ready for this. He stood up, face-to-face with Rajan. "I know who you are and I know how powerful you are. Believe me, this is the last thing I want to be doing now. I want to find out who killed your brother's son. Right now, I am your best hope. You can either answer my questions, let me eliminate you as a suspect or you can continue to antagonise me; make me waste all of our time," said Gaurav sharply. He trusted Rajan would be wise and not vain. He hoped he was right.

Rajan was unfazed. He looked offended but he had heard all that Gaurav had to say. The policeman was right. As much as he wanted to knock him out on the spot, he would only be wasting time by doing that. He clicked his tongue and then decided to get it over with.

"Don't think that I am doing this for you. I am doing this for my boy. Gabbar was like a son to me. Everybody knows that. Feel free to question me but you are wasting your time," said Rajan as he sat down on his chair with his arms crossed.

Rajan was calm throughout the questioning. He was nowhere in the vicinity on the night of the murder. Though he had the power to get hired hands to do this, Gaurav had a gut feeling that he did not.

***

10:30 AM

Gaurav waited in Baldev Singh's office lobby. He did not have any proof linking Baldev Singh to the murder but he wanted to check the lead nevertheless. If Gun Baba had mentioned him, he was worth looking into. His office was simple and it was within the factory. He was surprised to see a policeman at his lobby and immediately called Gaurav in.

"How can I help you? May I know what this is about?" Baldev Singh asked calmly.

"This is just a simple questioning," said Gaurav.

"Questioning? Do I need a lawyer?" the man asked, looking cautious.

"I don't think so. I thought we could have a casual chat," said Gaurav.

"I've got an anticipatory bail already. You already know that it is not my fault, right? Even the labourers are on my side here," said Baldev Singh nervously.

"What are you talking about?" Gaurav asked.

"What is this about?" Baldev Singh asked, looking surprised. He relaxed a bit when he realised that Gaurav was not there about the thing that he feared it would be about.

"I wanted to talk to you regarding Gabbar's murder," said Gaurav.

"Oh," said Baldev Singh, heaving a sigh of relief. "Don't get me wrong. We had an accident in the factory six days ago. It was not our fault but a couple of influential people have been trying to take me down using it as a reason. I thought you were here regarding that."

"Do you know about Gabbar's murder?" Gaurav asked.

"Know it? I wanted to celebrate it. If not for this accident, I would be doing just that," said Baldev Singh with a grin. He looked at the bewildered expression on Gaurav's face. "Don't get me wrong. I did not have anything to do with it. You must have heard what he did to my son."

"I heard about that. You have good reason to want vengeance on him," said Gaurav.

"Do I need a lawyer?" Baldev Singh asked, looking nervous again.

"This is a casual conversation. If I am satisfied with what you say to me, we don't need anybody," said Gaurav.

The man took a long look at Gaurav and then picked up his phone. "Stella, get my son here," said Baldev Singh curtly. He kept looking away determinedly.

"Do we really need your son here?" Gaurav asked as a smart man entered the room.

"This is my older son, not the one Gabbar took," said Baldev Singh.

"Why do we need him?" Gaurav asked.

"He is my lawyer," said Baldev Singh proudly.

"Abhay Singh," said the young man who had

entered the room. He was quite young. Gaurav shook his hand and looked at the card he handed to him. It stated that he was an assistant to a famous lawyer in the city. "What is this about?" the young man asked.

"I'm here regarding the recent murder of Gabbar in the marina area. You must have watched the news," said Gaurav.

"Oh," said the man, looking at his father. He nodded at his father. "We are happy to answer any questions you want on that," said Abhay Singh calmly.

"I understand that he kidnapped your son," said Gaurav, turning to Baldev.

"He did. It was a while back. He was a merciless goon," said the man, looking down at his feet.

"You have reason for wanting vengeance," said Gaurav.

"You realise that we did not file a case for the kidnap?" Abhay asked calmly.

"What does that have to do with this?" Gaurav asked.

"We have enough reason to want him dead but we don't live in an ideal world. This city belongs to Rajan Bhai. That is exactly why we did not file a case. That is also why we would not even dream about vengeance," said Abhay sharply.

"You could have hired—" began Gaurav.

"We would then have to spend our entire lives checking our backs for retribution. We have moved on from it. We had to. Nobody opposes Rajan and lives peacefully," said Abhay.

Gaurav saw that the father and son were being honest. They were scared but not regarding the line of questioning. They were scared to be implicated in this matter. They were scared that Rajan would see it in the same way. They were not hiding it. They did not strike him as killers. Either that or they were very good actors.

"Just to check, can you let me know where you were on the date and time of the murder?" Gaurav asked. He showed them his notes about the date and time of the murder.

"He was in the police station regarding the accident in the factory. It was routine questioning. We have not been charged with anything. The case should be closed soon and my father will be declared innocent. I was in with my boss going over this case. You can check this with him. He is one of the most reputed lawyers in the city," said Abhay, handing Gaurav his boss' card.

Gaurav was almost convinced that they had nothing to do with this but he got their contact information and their alibi details noted. He knew that there was a very slim chance that he would meet these two people again.

***

2:30 PM

"Is the woman here?" Gaurav asked as he entered the police station.

"Yes, she is," said Siddique.

"You can take the rest of the day off. This should be routine. You need rest," said Gaurav. The sub-inspector was injured and he needed the rest.

"No, sir. I would like to assist in every way possible to solve this case. I am alright," he said with a grin.

Gaurav smiled at him and shook his head as he turned away. Siddique was thinking that this was a commendation. He was taking pride in working more. Gaurav remembered when he used to be like this. It took him a long time to realise the reality of his situation.

They reached the next room where a petite woman was waiting for them. She was dressed in simple clothes but looked attractive. She didn't seem like she was grieving. She looked scared to be in the police station. A lot of people were eyeing her and that was making her visibly uncomfortable. She sat cross-legged in a corner, looking around nervously.

"Siddique, we called her in for questioning. Why did you put her near the cells? The poor woman looks terrified," said Gaurav, beckoning her. The woman hesitated for a moment and then followed him. He noticed her attractive hazel eyes as she passed him.

"Don't worry. We only want to ask you a few questions," said Siddique to the woman politely.

The woman entered the interrogation room. She looked calmer than before. She became comfortable once they switched on the fan. Siddique stood near the door as Gaurav sat opposite the woman. She looked anxious again on seeing Gaurav. He smiled at her reassuringly but it did not seem to put her at ease.

"You are Angel? Blade is your brother, right?" Gaurav asked as he looked at the file with details on the case.

"Yes, Blade was my brother," said Angel nervously.

"Do you know who had a reason to kill your brother?" Gaurav asked.

"I don't know. He was Gabbar's henchman. A lot of people wanted him dead for a lot of reasons," she said.

"You don't seem very shaken by the news," said Gaurav sharply.

"Do you want me to be crying now?" Angel asked with a scowl. Her initial fear was slowly ebbing away.

"That would be the natural reaction," said Gaurav.

"We weren't that close and I have spent the entire night crying my heart out. I did not wish for his death but I do not have any affection for him either," said Angel.

"Why?" Gaurav asked.

"Personal reasons," said the woman, turning away.

"Does this have to do with Gabbar?" Gaurav asked.

"Everything in our sad and cursed life had to do with Gabbar. This is no exception," said the woman.

"Can you tell us what was the nature of your relationship with Gabbar?" Siddique asked, looking at her intently.

"You did not ask me if I know him," said the woman as she frowned at Siddique.

"Do you?" Gaurav asked.

"I do and whatever you must have heard is true," said the woman calmly.

"What do you think we have heard?" Siddique asked.

"You must have heard that I am Gabbar's mistress. I was," said the woman.

"You are not anymore?" Gaurav asked.

"Things have changed," said the woman, leaning back in her chair. The woman was calm as she spoke about her position. She did not seem apologetic about it.

"What happened?" Gaurav asked.

"I got pregnant thrice. My brother forced me to abort the baby twice. Gabbar found out the last time. Gabbar lost interest after that. He had had other interests since. He came around sometimes but not like before," said the woman.

"You don't seem worried that he is dead," said Siddique sharply.

"He was not my husband. He had me for one thing only. Once he got bored, he moved on. He still had me around but it was not like before," said the woman indifferently.

"Did that anger your brother?" Siddique asked, sitting down next to Gaurav. Gaurav decided to let him take the lead in the questioning. Siddique was overzealous but he was going in the right direction.

"He was but not in the way you think," said Angel.

"What do you mean?" Siddique asked, looking at Gaurav.

"Gabbar had the decency to tell me that he was screwing me. My brother did not even have that," she said.

"Did he—?" Siddique began awkwardly.

"Not like that. Blade brought me here from our village for the sole reason of pimping me out to Gabbar. He used my position to make more money and get closer to Gabbar. He would not have minded pimping me out to others but this simply was more profitable for him," said Angel.

"Profitable?" Siddique asked, looking surprised.

"My brother wanted to settle down in life. He saw this as an opportunity and grabbed it immediately," said Angel, looking disgusted. She waited for a moment and shook her head angrily. "There is a new shopping complex coming up at the end of the marina. Since Gabbar was with me, my brother used that to his advantage. He got a shop there. He was going back to our village to sell our small piece of land to start a shop," she said.

"He was going to leave Gabbar?" Siddique asked, looking at Gaurav again.

"He would not have left Gabbar. This is not a job where you can quit. The end of this kind of a job is death or prison. Gabbar was going to be in our lives forever. Blade was going to milk that and get as much money out of this as possible. I am still young and my brother's greed had no limit," said Angel sadly.

"He had no reason to kill Gabbar?" Siddique asked.

"I don't know if he had reason but he did not have the guts. My brother was no saint. He was worse than Gabbar. He forced me to have abortions just to avoid the risk of Gabbar losing his interest in me. The world is not any worse without him in it. I'm happy he died. I'm not happy how it happened but I am happy that he died," said Angel.

"You can leave now but stick around in case we need to ask you further questions," said Gaurav.

"Let me go at the earliest. I am planning to sell the shop and go back to our village. Gabbar is gone and so is my brother. I can finally try and have a normal life," said Angel.

"We'll keep that in mind but I want you to inform us where and when you go," said Gaurav, walking out of the room. Siddique got her to sign a few statements before letting her go. When he finished with her and returned to the meeting room, the DCP was in the room with them.

"What do you think of Angel?" Gaurav asked.

"I don't know exactly but I am inclined to say that she is our best suspect as of this moment," said Siddique. Gaurav did not think so but he remained silent.

"Give me a break! A weak little girl killed Gabbar and her own brother in such a brutal fashion?" the DCP asked.

"We need more information. She is our best suspect because she has an emotional motive. There is so much that we do not know. Gabbar had many enemies but most of them could not have pulled this off. It had to be someone in the area. Angel had motive to kill both Gabbar and Blade. Siddique is right on that point. Based on the way these people were killed, she could not have done it alone," said Gaurav.

"A lover perhaps or another family member?" Siddique asked.

"That is where it stops making sense. Nobody in that area would dare to be involved with Angel. Gabbar kept her on the down low but he would not have been fine with anyone even getting near that girl," said Gaurav.

"What do you mean? Is she not a suspect now?" Siddique asked.

"This guy, Hemant," said Gaurav, throwing a photo on the table. Gaurav had done his research well. He had done his work on identifying every person in Gabbar's inner circle. The other policemen were more concerned with the bodies but Gaurav was more interested in where each person was. Once he had spoken to Angel, it was clear.

This man had been missing since the night Gabbar

had died. He and Blade were always around Gabbar. Gaurav had been expecting his body to show up just like Blade but this made more sense. Hemant was from the area, close to Gabbar and he had access. Angel was beautiful and beautiful women could make men do the silliest of things.

"This guy? I don't think so," said Siddique, looking at his photograph.

"Let's find out, shall we?" Gaurav asked as he stepped out of the room. He saw Siddique follow him and raised his hand to stop him. "I want you here. If we find this guy and he turns out to be the one, we are going to have to chase him down. You are in no position to chase him," said Gaurav.

"I can take care of myself," said Siddique, looking disappointed.

"You have done well, Siddique. You are supposed to be on medical leave. I appreciate you even being here. If you feel like you have to work, there is paperwork," said Gaurav, pointing to the room.

"You are going to the marina now?" Siddique asked.

"No. I am going to find the patrol officers from that night. If this guy was arrested that night, we don't need to bother with the chase," said Gaurav.

"I can help," said Siddique.

"Yes. Help me with the paperwork," said Gaurav, pointing to the room. Siddique walked away sadly. Gaurav smiled to himself. He put the over-enthusiastic sub-inspector out of his mind and went in search of the patrol officer from that night.

***

3:25 PM

Digant Sharma, a fifty-year-old head constable from the patrol unit was new to the area. He had a long career without much development. He had been stationed near the marina that night along with a couple of other officers.

A few minutes after leaving Siddique, Gaurav was in the car with Krishna and two other constables in mufti on the way to where Digant Sharma was on duty. He had picked people who could chase Hemant if he did not come in quietly. They found the policeman exactly where they were told he would be. The slightly-obese man was sitting under a tree with two other policemen, having lunch.

"Good afternoon," he said, getting up on his feet seeing Gaurav.

"Please sit. I just need a little help. It can wait till you are done with your food," said Gaurav politely.

"I can have it later, Sir. How can I help?" Digant asked.

"We can wait till you eat. Nothing is that urgent," said Gaurav kindly.

"Would you like some rotis? We have enough to

share," said Digant humbly.

"I'd love some," said Gaurav with a smile. He was hungry. Without his wife, he had forgotten to make food for himself. Taking the old head constable on his offer proved to be a blessing. The food was delicious. As they had food, Digant Sharma eased up and gave him all the details he needed.

He was well-organised and knew all the details that Gaurav wanted. Hemant had been with Gabbar for more than a decade. On that night, he had been detained too. After a few minutes, he had asked Digant permission to go after Gabbar as he looked too drunk for his own good.

"You let him go? Just like that?" Gaurav asked. He tried to be casual in his chat. He knew that the police in the area gave a long leash to Rajan's gang members. It was not worth the trouble unless it was an important case.

"I am told that you used to work this area. Would you have held these boys for a simple charge like that?" Digant asked.

"I understand. I've been looking for this guy. He is a suspect," said Gaurav.

"For what?" Digant asked, looking surprised.

"Gabbar's murder," said Gaurav.

"No way. Are you serious?" Digant asked, looking bemused.

"We are. We have good reason," said Gaurav.

"That boy was no saint. He did every bad thing in the book but he would never harm Gabbar. He worshipped him," said Digant.

"Right now, he is our best suspect. We haven't found him so far to question him. He was absent during Gabbar's funeral, my men have informed me," said Gaurav.

"I don't know about that but I don't think he is hiding," said Digant.

"How can you be so sure?" Gaurav asked.

"I am looking at him," said Digant, pointing behind Gaurav. A few hundred feet away, there was an abandoned car on the roadside. Crouching next to it and smoking a cigarette was a dark and medium-built man. "That is the Hemant you are looking for," said Digant.

Just as they were looking at him, Hemant turned towards them. He looked a little hungover. It took him a few seconds to see that a policeman was pointing at him. Gaurav quickly turned to look at the constables who had accompanied him. They did not need to be told.

They understood Gaurav and began to walk towards Hemant at a brisk pace. They had reduced the distance between them and the suspect by half when Hemant realised what was happening. He turned around and began to sprint.

Gaurav sighed as he stood up. He did not want to go on a chase now; he hadn't even had water after eating the rotis. He began to run towards the suspect.

Hemant had been surprised by them but he was a good runner. He was increasing the distance between him and his pursuers steadily. He knew the area well and he was agile and nimble footed.

He was picking corners to confuse them and it was difficult to keep him in their sight. Within the first five minutes, Gaurav realised that this was not going to be easy. The constables were nowhere in sight and he was not sure where he was. He had reached a small street that led to three alleys. He had no idea which one to take. He took his wireless and hoped that the constables had taken theirs too.

"Report position, over," he said as he looked around.

"Near the wine shop. Lost the suspect, over," came one of the voices immediately.

As they kept speaking on the wireless, Gaurav saw Hemant. He was crouching and panting with his head between his knees. Gaurav could not see either of his companions nearby. He began to walk cautiously towards Hemant, not wanting to alert him. Hemant realised it too late.

He looked at Gaurav as though he had given up. His eyes widened as he took a step back. Gaurav was less than five feet away when Hemant broke into a sprint. Gaurav was gaining on him and had almost grabbed him when Hemant turned and pushed him.

Both Gaurav and Hemant fell to the ground. Gaurav

crawled forward and tried to pin him to the ground but Hemant escaped his hold. Gaurav got kicked in his face. Gaurav aimed a punch on his shin and followed that with a couple more to his thigh. Once he found his mark, he clutched his face and rolled over.

He could hear Hemant groan as he lay clutching his leg, but he got up to his feet fast. Gaurav resumed pursuit but Hemant had turned a corner and disappeared from sight. Gaurav kicked the ground with disgust. He had lost his man. He looked around for a proper vantage point to spot the accused.

"He can't have gotten too far," said Gaurav on the wireless as he climbed the stairs to reach the terrace of the tall building near him.

"I'm moving west, over," said the constable from near the wine shop.

"Mic two, report your position, over," said Gaurav as he reached the terrace. Gaurav looked around. He had a good vantage from there. He could see a large part of the marina. Most of the area looked quiet. When someone was running, you could usually see it from the reaction of the people in the surroundings. Gaurav wished he had a pair of binoculars. It was difficult to see what was happening.

"Mic two, report," said Gaurav as he noticed something below. He noticed the suspect's shirt from his position. He was moving slowly with no pursuers behind him. "I see him. He is near the barber shop near the playground. Lead him towards the edge of the slum. I want as few witnesses as possible," said Gaurav.

"Mic two reporting. I see him. Starting pursuit," said the voice.

"Finally!" Gaurav said as he ran towards the edge of the slum. He wanted to do this quietly. Any attention to this in this area would create a lot of problems. Firstly, it would not be quiet. Secondly, Rajan and his gang would want the man for themselves and it would result in a bloodbath.

"Mic one reporting. I am in pursuit but he is entering the small streets," said a voice on the wireless.

"Mic two reporting. I lost sight of him," said the other voice.

Gaurav sighed as he clutched his face. This was beyond their control now. Many would have learned about this by now and Hemant would be killed if they did not catch him. "Come in, all units," he said, changing the frequency. "Units, respond," he said as he kept checking the frequency.

"Emergency riot squad head constable Salim reporting, over," came a voice.

"Salim, we are in pursuit of a suspect near the barber shop in the marina. Suspect is a balding man, dark and medium-built with a dark green T-shirt. We lost him heading north from there. We need to do this quick and clean," said Gaurav quickly.

"We will be there in a couple of minutes. Do you

have anyone else in the area?" Salim asked as he began instructing his team about the pursuit.

"Two constables are on his tail. We need to do this quickly or there will be tension in the area," said Gaurav.

Gaurav began to listen to the wireless and kept changing his course based on it. The riot squad was a great help. Seeing Hemant run, people in the area got alerted and began to follow them. The riot squad was keeping away unnecessary elements from interfering. With numbers on their side, they were getting closer.

Hemant was entering a building under construction. They were surrounding the building when Gaurav reduced his pace. They had contained the situation. All he needed to do was take Hemant in quietly and get the rest of the events confirmed by his confession.

"Mic two reporting. Sir, we have a problem," said the voice.

"What happened? Does he have any hostages?" Gaurav asked, concerned.

"Worse. He fell off the top of the building," said the voice.

"Damn it," said Gaurav as he sprinted towards the building. There were thirteen men in total including the two men he had got with him. The building was among the many being constructed by the housing board for the fishermen in the area. Hemant had fallen off the edge of the building onto a stockpile on the ground. He had fallen on iron rods and died on the spot.

Gaurav walked up to the spot and looked at where he had fallen. He had wanted to take the man alive but he did not have any problem with what had happened. The angle of the fall did not look like he had slipped. It looked odd but fear made people move unpredictably. He had to get the scene cleaned up and explain the whole fiasco to the DCP. He dialled his number even as he dreaded the conversation.

CHAPTER 8

FINDING ANGEL

A few miles away, Angel was walking back to her house. The men in Angel's life had never treated her properly. Her father was a drunk who beat her and her mother many times. Her mother had committed suicide when she could not tolerate him anymore. She did not even get to complete her schooling. She liked school and had many dreams. None of them came true.

Her brother was worse. He was greedy and did not hesitate to pimp her to Gabbar. He took any money that she managed to hide. It was always about him. She had no fond memories of Gabbar but he was better than the men in her family. There were times when he had made her feel good but that was lost in a sea of bad moments.

"I bear the child of a monster in a world that has given me no hope. What am I going to do with you? They say that if I kill you, I will never be able to have another child. Is that such a bad thing?" Angel asked as she rubbed her stomach. She was beginning to show.

Walking back from the station, she felt relieved and free. All her tormentors were now dead.

Perhaps life will be different for you. We will not let pigs dictate our lives. We will go away from all this evil and try to be happy, she thought as she walked faster. A couple of cars stopped dangerously close to her. She did not know who the men were but she was sure that they were from Gabbar's gang.

"We don't want to hurt you. Come with us," said one of the men. He revealed a knife and signalled her to come quietly.

Angel knew that she had no choice. Screaming in this area would make no difference. She got into one of the cars quietly and expected to be taken somewhere in the outskirts to be dealt with. The car sped along the marina but surprisingly, she was taken towards Rajan's house. She kept quiet as the car came to a halt. The other men in the car were determinedly staring away. She had seen a few of them with her brother.

"What is this about?" she asked one of the men she knew.

"Rajan Bhai wants to meet you," said the man, looking terrified.

Angel exited the car slowly. She had never been to Rajan's house. Gabbar used to live here too. There were many people in and around the house. She followed a man who gestured to her. The house looked beautiful and neat. Everything was in its place. There were no expensive items but it felt nice. Angel lost a bit of fear after entering the house. She passed the huge hall where almost a dozen people were being served food. She passed the room without making eye-contact with anyone.

After walking for a few minutes, she found herself on the terrace. Rajan was sitting with his wife at a distance but she was made to stand facing Baaji. She had never met him in person. He was an older and shorter version of Gabbar but he was scarier. Angel stared at the floor.

"You were with my son?" Baaji asked gruffly.

"Yes," said Angel softly.

"Gabbar found out about your pregnancy the second time but you told the police that he got you pregnant thrice," said Baaji.

"Yes," said Angel, looking bewildered. She wondered how they knew but realised that this was Rajan's family. They had people everywhere. Nothing stayed a secret, even what was discussed in police stations.

"The third time, you still carry the child?" Baaji asked.

Angel looked around and saw the other men staring at her. She felt humiliated. She could not accept or deny in the presence of so many men. She hung her head in shame.

"You guys can leave," said Baaji. The men obeyed meekly. Baaji became more pleasant once the men left. "Sit," he said but it was not an order. It was almost a request. Angel sat down reluctantly. "Did my son got you pregnant again?" Baaji asked, almost being polite. From the corner of her eyes, she could see Rajan and his wife eyeing them intently.

"Yes," said Angel nervously.

"Stop being scared. If I wanted to harm you, we would not be having a conversation," said Baaji. "Do you still have the child?"

"My brother had me abort immediately," said Angel nervously. She did not know how he would respond if he knew the truth. She cleared her throat and said, "Yes, Gabbar got me pregnant. My brother did not want to lose Gabbar's favour. He forced me to abort the child each time," she said, touching her stomach.

"How long have you been with him?" Baaji asked. He was not angry with the girl anymore. He tried to smile but that scared her even more.

"Almost two years," said Angel. She wondered if she had to feign tears to keep him satisfied but she did not even feel sad.

"Have you been with anyone—?" Baaji began awkwardly.

"Just Gabbar. I am not that kind of a girl," said Angel immediately. Something about the question irked her. She did not care what Baaji thought about her. She was his son's mistress but she did not want him to think of her as a woman of questionable morals. She had been forced into this life by her brother.

"Did he treat you well?" Baaji asked, sitting opposite to her. He looked apologetic about questioning the woman like this.

"What?" Angel asked, taken aback. It was shocking to see Baaji be so polite. She had heard a lot about him. She did not know that he even had a human side. "He treated me ok," said Angel.

"Your brother was Blade?" Baaji asked, leaning back in his chair.

"Yes," said Angel.

"Bastard! He told you to kill your child three times? What kind of a brother was he!" Baaji said.

"Twice. He died before I told him about—" said Angel slowly.

Baaji got off his chair and grabbed her arm. Rajan and his wife rushed towards them. Before they could reach him, Baaji was face-to-face with her. The strangest thing happened. Baaji was in tears. He held her hands in his.

"You bear my son's child now?" he asked, looking overwhelmed. Rajan and his wife stopped a few feet away from them. Rajan looked tense but his wife was relieved. "You hear that, Rajan?" Baaji asked his brother.

"Are you sure?" Rajan asked, raising his eyebrows.

"I have been pregnant before. Of course, I am sure," began Angel hotly. It was ridiculous that a man was asking her if she was sure that she was pregnant.

"I don't think she is lying," said Rajan's wife,

looking at her husband. Rajan looked at her with a curious expression but he did not speak further. "I am sure she is not lying," said Rajan's wife.

Baaji used both his arms to hold her cheeks. It was not rough like when he had grabbed her arm. He was gentle and almost seemed affectionate. The powerful don was now in tears. "I know that my son did not treat you the way you deserved to be treated. I know that I have no right to ask you this. But will you have his child? I will treat you like my own daughter for the rest of your life," said Baaji expectantly.

"I don't—" began Angel nervously.

"We will treat you like family. You can choose to stay with us or I will help you live the life you want. We will take very good care of you. We will be your family," said Baaji, stuttering as he spoke.

"Please accept, my dear," said Rajan softly. He placed a hand firmly on his brother's shoulder, pulling him back. "We will treat you as family like my brother promised. We will give you anything you want and that is my promise."

Angel looked at Baaji, who looked at her hopefully. She did not want to agree to what he was asking but she felt like she did not have a choice in the matter. The thought of aborting another child terrified her. This way, she would have a family and be provided for. She would never be one of them but it would still be better than the family she had with her brother. She nodded slowly.

Baaji looked at her approvingly and placed his hand on her to bless her. “From this day forward, you are my daughter,” he said warmly.

Angel realised that there was no turning back from this. Rajan’s wife smiled at her but Rajan had a blank expression. He looked like he did not completely trust her. It did not matter. She knew that it would take time. She did not know what the future held for her but she knew that she would be comfortable for the next few months under the care of the most powerful man in the city.

***

5:30 PM

“We can’t find Angel,” said Siddique, throwing his hands up in dismay.

“What do you mean? They had her address,” said Gaurav.

“Her house is locked. She seems to have left in a hurry. I enquired,” said Siddique.

“I don’t believe it. She made a run for it?” Gaurav asked, dialling the DCP on his phone. “Put your arm in the sling, Siddique. You won’t heal otherwise,” said Gaurav as he waited for the DCP to answer his phone. He waited for a couple of minutes but it kept ringing. Just as he ended the call, he got another call from a different number.

"This is Rajan. I want to talk to you. Could you please come over to my place?" Came the voice on the other side.

"Rajan? Which Rajan?" Gaurav asked, with very little doubt about the identity of the caller.

"You know which one. You also know my house. I hear you were searching for a girl named Angel," he said.

"You know where she is?" Gaurav asked hopefully.

"Come over as soon as possible," said Rajan, ending the call. Gaurav looked at the phone with disgust. He hated how Rajan treated the police. A few minutes later, he was in his car with Krishna and Siddique, going towards Rajan's house.

"Last time we went there, we asked him if he had murdered Gabbar," said Gaurav to Siddique nervously.

"The DCP said you were smart," said Krishna sarcastically.

"Not one of my best moments," said Gaurav.

"Is he going to have you beaten?" Krishna asked snidely.

"If he wanted to do that, he would do it in public. Besides, Rajan knows that grudges are pointless and that I was doing my job," said Gaurav.

"You do realise that Rajan is a gangster, right?" Krishna asked with a smile.

"This is not about me. He wanted to talk about Angel," said Gaurav quickly.

"Do you think he had her killed?" Siddique asked doubtfully.

"If he did, I don't think he would tell you," said Krishna. Gaurav remained silent. Rajan wouldn't mind gloating about a murder but something did not fit. As he sat thinking, they reached Rajan's house. They were led to the terrace where Rajan awaited them. He seemed to be in a good mood.

"That was fast," said Rajan as he gestured towards the empty chair in front of him. He had tea and biscuits brought up. Gaurav accepted it awkwardly but was surprised to see Angel holding the plate. She did not smile but she was not scared. "I heard you were looking for Angel. The boys told me that you were asking around her house. Should you feel the need to speak to her, this is where you will find her," said Rajan with a chuckle.

"We wanted to question her," began Siddique nervously but Gaurav quickly held his hand. The sub-inspector stopped talking immediately.

"Why is she here?" Gaurav asked politely.

"They did not make it public but she was married to Gabbar. Public or not, that makes her family. My brother insisted that she remain with us as part of our family. We lost a son but we have a daughter now," said Rajan calmly.

"Oh," said Gaurav, taken by surprise.

"She bears his child, you see. She lost her brother

too. We are the only family she has now. I could not let her be on the streets," said Rajan.

Gaurav looked at the woman who was now calmer than before. He smiled weakly. Siddique made no effort to hide his surprise.

"We just wanted to check if she was safe. There is no need for any questioning," said Gaurav quickly.

"You can go," said Rajan sweetly. Angel walked away towards the other corner where Rajan's wife sat with her kids. Rajan's wife was cordial with Angel and that surprised Gaurav. He looked at Siddique pointedly. It was an expression of protest but he walked away without saying anything.

"You believe that the child is his?" Gaurav asked bluntly, once he was sure that their conversation was private. He could not believe that Rajan believed the girl.

"Baaji wants to believe it. I don't think the girl is lying. Right now, my brother needs this," said Rajan. Gaurav looked at him with a suspicious expression. "I believe in things that are real. I will keep her close and raise the child as our own regardless. I will also get a DNA test done to confirm her words," said Rajan in an undertone.

"If the test fails?" Gaurav asked reluctantly.

"It won't. I have enough reason to trust the girl. Even if she fails the test, the child stays with us," said Rajan.

"The girl?" Gaurav asked.

"If she speaks the truth, she will become a part of my family. If not, she will be treated as what she is. I will throw money at her and make her go away if she has lied. The child will stay with us and Baaji will be none the wiser," said Rajan.

"You are fine with Baaji raising another man's child?" Gaurav asked.

"He lost his wife a long time back. Gabbar was everything to him. Why should he not have this?" Rajan asked. Rajan stepped up and walked closer. "This is my business. I will handle it. What about yours? Have you found the killer?" Rajan asked.

"The DCP did not tell you?" Gaurav asked, trying to stay calm.

"You think Hemant did this?" Rajan asked.

"The department does," said Gaurav.

"What do you think?" Rajan asked.

Gaurav remained quiet. He did not want to say anything stupid. "I am here only to prevent a war. The investigation is in the hands of better people," he said quickly.

Rajan smiled. He knew that Gaurav was lying but it did not matter. He knew that there would be no war now. Baaji would be pacified and the police would resume their business. He could find and kill the actual killer on his own. He smiled and left DSP Gaurav on his terrace. The policemen could find their way out. Rajan had to keep his eyes and ears open now.

CHAPTER 9

VENGEANCE MUST BE COMPLETE

7:00 PM

Gaurav kept looking at the evidence. The DCP wanted to close the case saying that Hemant was the killer. His death was inconvenient but with plenty of witnesses saying that it was an accident, the department would be in no trouble. It suited their requirements. Hemant being the killer would absolve the other gangs of any blame.

That meant that the police had to watch only Rajan for a short while before closing the case. The city would be quiet again and the law minister could claim a huge win. The media was covering the news with great vigour. They were talking about the heroics of the police in conducting the investigation and the dangerous chase. The more Gaurav saw the news, the more he began to doubt the man's intent. Hemant was a convenient suspect but he was not a perfect one.

It did not fit. Hemant did not come across as someone who could have beaten two of his friends to death. He was strong but Gaurav doubted the intent.

There was very little possibility that he could have taken on Gabbar, even a drunk one. If Hemant was dead and Blade was alive, he would not have this doubt.

Blade was capable and ambitious. Gaurav had been kicked by him. The man was small and he did not have the power to beat someone to death. Not alone. The affair with Angel angle made sense but he still had doubts.

"Siddique! Don't carry that with your arm like this," said Gaurav sharply as he saw the sub-inspector carry a box of files and photos to his room.

"There was nobody else," said Siddique.

"You are in a station full of policemen. Don't be a hero. Let your arm heal," said Gaurav sternly. "You can go home now," he added kindly, seeing the man look hurt.

"The case?" Siddique asked.

"The media has their guy. We have to stick to it now," said Gaurav.

"Are we convinced it is him?" Siddique asked.

"Convinced or not, I am finishing the paperwork. I should be back at my regular job next week," said Gaurav.

"You don't have to do all the paperwork. I can pick it up," he said kindly.

"I know but I like doing this. Sometimes, it helps me get a proper perspective. Don't worry about me. I am happy to do this," said Gaurav.

"Most people hate paperwork," said Siddique.

"They do because they don't realise what it offers. Nobody has time to think about a case properly. We all want to close cases. When I do the paperwork, I rethink the case. I have found my mistakes and corrected them by doing paperwork," said Gaurav proudly.

The sub-inspector walked to the door and turned to Gaurav just before he left the room. "It was nice working with you," said Siddique.

"It was the same for me too. All the best for the rest of your career, Siddique," said Gaurav as he closed the door and turned his attention to the case details.

He went over the entire incident. On the day of his murder, Gabbar was drunk and was travelling with a few of his men. Police had apprehended them but let Gabbar go. A few minutes later, they allowed Hemant to follow him. People had seen Gabbar pass through the slum but nobody had seen Hemant.

He was only five minutes behind Gabbar. Gabbar's detour was out of his normal path, which could explain why nobody saw Hemant that night. If he had somehow passed through the slum and beaten Gabbar to death, there was no reason to hang around the slum. On the other hand, Hemant was not at the scene when the police found the body.

Gaurav had checked the photos. He wished he could have questioned his whereabouts before he fell to his death. He had no way to confirm it now. Everyone wanted to believe that it was Hemant. There was circumstantial evidence against him. The case was closed and the danger of a gang war was diminishing.

It was also convenient as the suspect could not defend himself. The charge sheet was ready and the paperwork was done. Gaurav was reluctant to close the file but this meant that he could go on vacation and be with his kids.

Gaurav walked up to the DCP's cabin. The case had ended abruptly but he had decided long ago that family came first. The sooner he got home, the better it was for him.

***

10:30 PM

Baaji was seething with anger. His son had been killed and he never even got to confront the killer. The police had made a mess of it. He had no love lost for Hemant but he could not help but regret that he had not killed him. He had wanted to kill his son's murderer by his own hands. He wanted to take his time and torture him to death for what he did to his boy. Gabbar was his son.

He had his shortcomings but he was still his son. The boy was obedient and respectful. Nothing else mattered. Rajan had said right from the start that they would kill Gabbar's murderer and that this would not end in court. Even Rajan had been surprised by the turn of events.

Rajan had mentioned that they had to find who ordered the kill. He was certain that even if Hemant had killed Gabbar, he got the order from someone else. This person was a threat to everything they had. Rajan wanted him dealt with.

"It is the writer," said one of his men, handing him his phone. The writer in the nearby police station was their spy in the department. He usually gave them very good information but he had been late in informing them about Hemant. The delay had caused Hemant to escape from being killed by Baaji. This was the second time he was calling that day.

"What does he want now?" Baaji asked angrily.

"He wants to talk to you," said the man quietly.

"What?" Baaji asked rudely as he answered the phone.

"Bhai, there is nobody powerful enough on the street claiming Gabbar's murder," said the writer, sounding nervous.

"You called me to tell me that?" Baaji asked angrily.

"Do you know Isaac from Cyrus' gang?" the writer asked.

"He is a wimp. What about him?" Baaji asked.

"He has told people that he arranged this," said the writer.

"What about Cyrus?" Baaji asked, getting curious.

"He hasn't said a word. He has been extremely quiet. I asked around and it looks like only Isaac speaks of this," said the writer.

"That wimp killed my son? There is no way. He is not that smart," said Baaji.

"Isaac approached some hitmen around that time. I don't have the exact details yet but the DSP had something in his notes. Rajan Bhai told me to let him know if I heard anything," began the writer but Baaji ended the call.

Baaji swore loudly and banged the table near him. He kicked the table multiple times. His foot hurt but he did not care. He could not get his head around what he had just heard. Isaac was not capable of doing something like this. Gabbar would have seen him coming from a mile away. Cyrus was capable but he would want the credit for something as big as this.

He knew that Cyrus wanted revenge for his father's murder but Baaji had no part in it. Gabbar definitely had no part in it. Baaji knew that Cyrus blamed everyone for it. His gang operated just to spite everyone else. Baaji paced around, thinking about Cyrus when it struck him. Isaac must have lied.

Cyrus was not strong, so calling hitmen made sense. Isaac was an old fool who was not capable of this but he was loyal. He was loyal enough to make the arrangements for this. Cyrus must have done it and got cold feet after. He wanted someone to take the fall for it when he was exposed and this was Isaac making himself useful.

"I want to know where we can find Cyrus," said Baaji to one of his men.

"He will be in the market now. He is untouchable there," said the man solemnly.

"There is nowhere in this city where I cannot touch him. I am finishing him!" Baaji said seriously.

"That is impossible," said the man.

"Did you forget who I am? Or are you drunk?" Baaji asked menacingly.

"Bhai, he will be in the market. He will be surrounded by his men. It is going to take a lot of manpower to bring him down," said the man nervously.

"Is that supposed to scare me?" Baaji asked sarcastically.

"We need a plan. We cannot go in just like that," said the man, looking nervous.

"We won't. This is not something I have just planned. I have been wanting to finish him off for quite a long time. This seems like the perfect opportunity," said Baaji confidently.

"Should I tell Rajan?" another man asked.

"You will tell nobody. We are doing this now. I want your phones switched off. We finish this before we do anything else," said Baaji angrily. His men did not protest. They would do anything for him without question.

***

1:45 PM (THE NEXT DAY)

Isaac walked around the central market area to collect the tributes from the shops. It was called 'protection money' when they were paid by the shopkeepers. The central market was a happening place. It ensured steady business. People joked that it was a place where one could take junk to sell but still walk out with a profit. With the certainty of making a sale, getting a shop space in the central market became expensive.

It had been built by the government for poor sellers. There were six hundred shops in the market area. One hundred were taken by benamis of politicians and corrupt officials. Out of the remaining five hundred, close to a hundred shops were given to poor sellers who were poor at that time.

Over the years, many of those people became comfortably rich. A few spaces were given to NGOs. One hundred more were politically motivated allocations. Different sections of vote-banks of different political parties were also favoured. After all this, almost two hundred and fifty shops were allocated on a monthly rental for individuals.

There was a process of issuing monthly tenders for these but Cyrus controlled all of these shops. He had also gained indirect control of the other shop spaces via strategic moves. The ones who were allocated the shops gave up resisting him and let him control their shop spaces for handsome monthly payments.

With political and official connections, nobody messed with them. It was easy money. It was an unbelievable amount of money from an unbelievable place. The tenders earned the government anywhere between ten thousand and fifteen thousand rupees based on the location of the shop. However, Cyrus got more than fifty thousand per month for each shop.

He could charge more for prime locations and even more during festive periods. In addition to the money, Cyrus had a lot of goodwill in the market. Both Rajan and Akhtar wanted the market. They had wanted it for years. Cyrus could have picked any spot as the base of his operations but he chose the central market simply to spite them.

Isaac had been with Cyrus's father. The man had been a moderately successful politician. Isaac believed that Cyrus would have been better than his father. His father's death had changed him. Cyrus had stepped away from politics to make vengeance his sole purpose in life. It had been years but he was no closer to getting his revenge.

He was no closer to finding the murderer now than he had been at the time of the death. Isaac had hoped that Cyrus would give up and go back to politics or something more respectable but Cyrus would not give up. He could not let it go.

"Come back later," said one of the shopkeepers rudely when Isaac approached him.

"What did you say to me?" Isaac asked loudly.

"Are you having a problem with your ear? I told you to come back later. I am busy," said the shopkeeper rudely. There was nobody in the shop and it was one of those dull days.

"You seem new. Perhaps you don't know who I am," said Isaac gravely.

"I know you and I know your father too. That doesn't change my answer. Go away now," he said in an insulting manner.

From the corner of his eye, Isaac saw the men from his gang on their feet, ready to pounce. He subtly signalled them to get back to their positions. This man had to be taught his place but this was not the right time. These were business hours and a beat down in public would only hurt morale. He smiled at the shopkeeper who had begun to bark instructions to his assistant. The shopkeeper would not walk the next day. Isaac grinned as he looked at the man's stupid face.

Isaac waited the rest of the day with the shop in his line of sight at all times. He had his lunch in one of the empty shops that gave him a view of the shopkeeper. Cyrus came to the spot and took a seat opposite to Isaac. He kept staring at the shop casually. He did not know how but Cyrus had heard of the incident.

He was someone who did not take disrespect easily. In their line of work, respect was everything. Cyrus wanted to be there for the beat down. It was dusk as they stood there, having tea. Most of the shops had begun to close. The arrogant shopkeeper still had his store open.

***

5:40 PM

"Who is this guy? I asked you to get his details," said Isaac to one of his lackeys.

"He is a spice seller. He paid a lot to get the store but he was an arrogant bastard even during the tender process. He is a miser and wanted a discount on the shop to start with. He has six days left in this shop," said one of the guys.

"He has nothing left anymore. He will be dealt with tonight and he will never step foot in my market again," said Cyrus angrily. Isaac loved this about Cyrus. He did not take a lot of time to decide.

"I think we can start now," said Isaac. There were hardly a dozen people in the entire row and most of them were leaving. The arrogant shopkeeper's assistant was away and he was listening to songs.

There were eight men with them as Cyrus and Isaac walked towards the shop. There was just one man in the shop. Isaac had the familiar thrill of the moments preceding a beating. He loved it when they taught people a lesson. A beating was the best way to get people in line. This was going to be a big one. Cyrus looked determined as he walked towards the shop.

The shop had a small assortment of cups filled with spices in the front for sampling and several bags of spices in the back. The shopkeeper did not know what hit him. Cyrus flung the contents of one of the cups on the unsuspecting shopkeeper who was whistling a tune with his eyes closed.

When he opened his eyes, there was not much time to react. Cyrus was sitting over him, punching his face in a matter of seconds. The man did not resist. There was no use fighting back. He was outnumbered and there was no upside to fighting back. He would only get beaten more or worse.

After about two minutes, Isaac stepped forward to place a hand on Cyrus's shoulder. "I think he has had enough," he said softly.

Cyrus let go of the man who dropped to the ground. He was panting as he was handed a cloth to wipe the blood on his knuckles.

"I think you should give it another go for a while, Cyrus," said the man on the ground with a bloody smirk.

"What did you say?" Cyrus asked angrily, aiming a kick at the man's groin.

The man groaned as he clutched his groin. His face was bloodied and his shirt was ripped in places. Isaac went close to the man to have a good look.

They had not noticed it until then but the whole

area had been too silent. Nobody had come hearing the commotion. It happened in a flash. The bags in the back of the shop had been in the dark for too long. Behind the bags, he could see a man's foot. Before he could warn anyone or even raise a voice, four men stepped out of the back of the bags. Each held a gun in their hand. Before he could even be shocked, they had begun to fire. After almost three minutes of continuous firing, the sound of bullets stopped.

Isaac was face-down on the ground. He had been shot and he was trapped under a chair on which one of their shooters sat. All their men had been gunned down. Cyrus lay on the ground a few feet away from him. He was alive but only just. He was resting his head on a bag of spices with a couple of bullet wounds in his abdomen.

"Cyrus!" Isaac called with tears. He could not bear to watch the boy in this position. "You cowards! You rotten cowards!" he shouted but the men did not care.

Cyrus lay on the ground. Unlike Isaac, he was not trapped. It did not matter. He would not get far. The shooters had finished everyone else but he was being kept alive. Just as he began to wonder why, he saw a group of men walk towards the shop. He squinted as everything looked hazy.

There was no mistaking it. Baaji walked with four men behind him. He had an impassive face as he came towards them. When he walked towards them, Cyrus knew it was all over. He turned to stare at Isaac who was pinned to the ground. Isaac was in tears seeing Cyrus. It was the tears which irked Cyrus. He could not comprehend how the old man could cry like a baby, giving their attackers the satisfaction of having beaten them.

"Cyrus," said Baaji gruffly as two men grabbed him and forced him to his knees.

"Baaji Bhai," said Cyrus weakly. He was not going to cry. He would not give Baaji that satisfaction. It took a lot of effort but he smiled confidently at the man.

"Why?" Baaji asked. His eyes were red.

Cyrus looked at Isaac. This had been his doing. He had taken the old man's stupid advice. Taking the heat for Gabbar's murder was always going to be risky. He realised now that he had grossly miscalculated and taken a needless risk.

"You made a mistake. You thought you were seeking vengeance. Vengeance. It cannot be in parts. It cannot be incomplete. You took," he said angrily as he punched hard on the floor. There was a lot of anger and sorrow in his face. "You took my boy away from me," he said weakly.

"We—" began Isaac weakly but one of the shooters kicked him in the mouth. Cyrus was thankful. He was going to die but this way, he would die having the satisfaction of wounding Baaji's pride.

"Did you kill my father?" Cyrus asked. He wanted to know. This could be the last thing he did in this life.

"Is that why you killed my boy?" Baaji asked. There was no anger in his face now. The man was grieving his son. That loss had hit him hard. He was conflicted by the whole conversation. He ran his finger over his facial scar and sighed sadly.

"Did you kill my father?" Cyrus repeated. He had to know.

"You should have killed me too. Vengeance must be complete. It cannot be half-baked. You should have finished all of us," said Baaji gravely.

"Did you kill my father?" Cyrus shouted desperately. He was going to die but he could not die without knowing.

"You killed my son," said Baaji curtly.

"I want to hear you say it! Say that you killed my father," screamed Cyrus. He wanted the man to admit it. He wanted the man to accept his crime.

Baaji closed his eyes and sighed. He signalled the men to let go. He took a gun and kept it pressed on one of the bullet wounds on Cyrus' abdomen. Cyrus tried hard not to wince. "If I had killed your father, you would not be here to seek vengeance. You fool! You killed my boy over nothing," said Baaji weakly.

Cyrus let go of the groan that he had suppressed all along. "Do you know who did?" he asked the man weakly.

Baaji emptied the entire gun into the man's stomach. He kept pulling the trigger long after the gun was empty. He kicked the body to the ground and began to stomp on the face of the corpse. As he vented his anger, his men finished Isaac. Every person associated with Cyrus and his gang had been killed in and around the market area.

CHAPTER 10

BREAKING NEWS

11:55 PM (TWO DAYS LATER)

Being the editor-in-chief of a national news channel had a lot of perks. Everybody knew who you were, you could dissect politicians on air, have talks with celebrities and have other people do all your research for you. As a data analyst for the said editor-in-chief, one had none of those perks.

The only thing you had was pressure. You had to get the facts straight, you had to cue the on-air shows and ensure that nothing came back to bite you later. It was an important job and came with a good salary but it was all risk and little reward.

Shrivali Sen was one of the best analysts in the top news channel of the country. When she went to college, she had no idea that she would end up here. She had been in this job for nearly four years now without taking a single day off. She had not been home for months but her parents had come over a few times.

Her job helped her afford a luxurious life but it came at the cost of her personal life. Shrivali woke up on her table at work, face-down on her keyboard. The document she had been working on had several pages of random letters now. She looked at the time. It was almost midnight.

"Three more hours and Mom will reach the airport," she said to herself sleepily and walked towards the coffee machine. There were only two other people in the office and both were from her team. Raj Mahavir Singh, her immediate junior, was flat on the floor and snoring loudly. He looked like the live version of Da Vinci's Vitruvian Man. Ebenezer, her teammate, was leaning on his chair and playing on his phone.

"Ebe, we have nothing for tomorrow. Stop playing your games and get to work. It is midnight already. I would like some sleep before tomorrow morning," said Shrivali angrily. Sipping her coffee, she lost some of the haziness in her sight. She had grown addicted to coffee. She couldn't function without it and her tolerance to it was rising every day.

"Something will turn up. It always does," said Ebenezer, lazily playing his game.

"Stop gaming and do your job. My mother is coming to visit me in a few hours and I would like to see her in person this time," said Shrivali angrily.

"Wait and watch. Something is definitely going to turn up. Did you check your mail?" Ebenezer asked.

"I have no mails in my inbox," said Shrivali, looking at her screen.

"Not your email. That new guy from the reception brought a few packages a few hours ago. It is on your desk. Check them. I trust your luck," said Ebenezer.

"Yeah. Pigs fly," said Shrivali as she sifted through her mail. "I see a package here with no stamps and no sender. It is just marked 'important' and plain otherwise," she said, looking curiously at the package.

"Be careful! It could be anthrax," said Ebenezer, taking his eyes away from his phone.

"Yeah, right! They leave all the important people and send it to us," said Shrivali sarcastically. Inside the box was a single DVD with 'watch me' written on it.

"You are not seriously thinking of playing that, are you?" Ebenezer asked, walking up to her with a puzzled expression.

"What's the worst that could happen?" Shrivali asked.

"It could be a computer virus that hacks into our system," said Ebenezer with a grin.

"I'd get a holiday at least," said Shrivali as she read the disc on her computer. There was a single video on it. Shrivali clicked on the video file and watched it with Ebenezer. They looked at each other with shock.

"Oh my god! We need to wake them up," said Ebenezer, staring at the video.

"Yeah, but who?" Shrivali asked.

"Everyone," said Ebenezer, looking at the disc. "Ask them to call the legal team too while you are at it," said

Ebenezer as he began to blow up the video.

***

3:00 AM

It was three hours after midnight and the newsroom was buzzing like it was primetime. Everyone was there in the office. Most of them were looking sleepy but they were determinedly staying awake. This was not a common occurrence.

Two days ago, there was a huge massacre in the central market. Cyrus and his entire gang had been murdered and every news outlet had stormed the area. The police did not have any clues but everyone knew who could have done such a thing. Baaji. There had been rumours going around that someone from Cyrus' gang had killed Gabbar. This was vengeance.

There was no proof but police were investigating from all angles for leads. They had taken Baaji and a few of his lieutenants in for questioning but they had got nothing to hold them. Baaji's lawyer had got him out on bail the same evening, which was somehow kept out of the news.

The video had the evidence that the police would need to make a case against Baaji. It had the complete footage of the entire murder. It was a fifteen-minute-long video shot from a distance. It clearly showed Baaji and his men executing Cyrus and nine other people in the middle of the market. It was brutal.

Ebenezer and Shrivali had watched the video multiple times to ensure that it had not been tampered with. It was not clear where the video was shot from. This was not one of the security cameras from the market. There was no clue who had shared the video but they knew that they were lucky. Finding a video like this was rare. This was going to be sensational.

“People! We have to go live with this. I hear that Rajeev’s team had it sent to their office as well,” said Sanjay, the editor-in-chief. He had a stack of papers in his hand while he was going through different ones.

“What? How did they get it?” Shrivali asked, looking surprised.

“Apparently, the video has been sent to every major news channel in the city and several print media. The police got a copy as well. We were the first ones to open it but everyone is informed. Most of them will air this for breakfast,” said Sanjay, looking grumpy.

Shrivali did not blame him. When he had come to the office earlier, he looked like he was offered an early bonus. Now, he looked furious. He did not like losing exclusive coverage.

“It doesn’t matter who breaks the news. This will get the police a conviction,” said Shrivali earnestly.

“I don’t give a damn about a conviction. I am not waiting until breakfast. We are breaking this in an hour. We will be the first to air this,” said Sanjay defiantly.

"Who watches the news so early?" Ebenezer asked, trying to be reasonable.

"The only thing that matters is what the news is. Trust me on this. This is news that people will wake up to watch. I want us ready to go live in thirty minutes," said Sanjay.

***

8:30 AM

Rajan knew where his brother was. He knew which hiding spot was the best. This place was known to very few and it was the safest place to hide from the police. Rajan was with Manish, his lawyer's assistant. He was part of the gang and Rajan's advisor. They had to think of a way to sort this out.

It was out in the media and almost impossible to control. None of what Manish was saying felt right to Rajan. Nobody knew Baaji's face outside the marina until now. Now, he was there on every channel. Even movie stars did not get this level of coverage.

"Baaji! What the hell did you do?" Rajan asked hotly as he reached his brother.

"What do you mean? I killed the lowlife who killed my son," said Baaji dismissively.

"You had to do it with lighting? In front of cameras? The murder is on every channel," shouted Rajan as he paced around.

"I don't know how that got into the news. I don't care. I killed the lowlife who killed my son," said Baaji angrily.

"Have you gone completely insane? Did your brain die when our boy was killed?" Rajan shouted angrily and smacked his brother on the head.

"Careful, brother! I will put you in the ground right now," warned Baaji.

"How could you be so foolish?" Rajan asked furiously as he clutched his hair.

"I did not know about the camera and I don't care," said Baaji.

"Not the camera, numbskull! Cyrus!" Rajan said, clicking his tongue.

"What about him?" Baaji asked.

"You really think that Cyrus could have laid a hand on our boy? He can't even aim properly while he pees. You thought he could even touch Gabbar in the middle of our area," said Rajan, sitting down with a grumpy expression.

"His lackey claimed the murder proudly," said Baaji.

"Like any wannabe would! He can't even guard his own area. Do you really think he can plan a sketch in ours? Do you ever think? You could have discussed this with me. Instead, you had to do something stupid and go viral," said Rajan, looking frustrated.

"No! He claimed it," said Baaji, shaking his head.

"He took credit because nobody else did," said Rajan loudly. "Isaac! Really? He is a petty shopkeeper. You bought his claim?" Rajan asked, throwing his hands up exasperatedly.

"How do you know they didn't do it?" Baaji asked, looking doubtful.

"We have been in this business for long enough to know that. We know what people are capable of," said Rajan, shaking his head and clicking his tongue.

"He thinks that we killed his father. We were involved. This could have been his way of getting back at us," said Baaji confidently.

"Nobody knows that except the two of us. We intended to keep it that way. Manish knows it now," said Rajan, pointing at the bewildered man.

"Manish will get me out. Won't you, Manish?" Baaji asked, turning towards Manish. He looked taken aback by being included in the conversation and shifted uneasily.

"Nobody can get you out of this for now. We are working on it. You have gone all out for killing a little boy who had nothing to do with all this," said Rajan.

"Who did it then?" Baaji asked. "I am fine with surrendering to the police but I will not go to jail knowing that the scum who killed my boy is still walking this earth," he said gravely.

"I will find out, brother. Gabbar was a son to me too. I want you to stay low. They are talking about an encounter for you," said Rajan.

"They are going to shoot me for this?" Baaji asked, looking at Manish.

"Your face is on every news channel. Did you have to do it personally?" Manish asked weakly.

"They killed my son," said Baaji angrily.

"I need you to lay low, Baaji Bhai. They want you done for this. It will take some negotiation to get them to even consider just arresting you," said Manish.

"That bad? Huh," said Baaji gruffly.

"Stay down. I have to figure out a way to keep you alive," said Rajan. If only it were that easy. He hugged his brother and patted his back before leaving the area.

"What do you think, Manish?" Rajan asked ten minutes later as they sat in the car.

"The minister wants to meet but it is going to be a lot of hard choices," said Manish.

Rajan sighed. He knew what Manish meant. He loved his brother but the minister would not see this from his point of view. Baaji was nobody to him. Rajan knew that he would like nothing about the discussion but he had to try. He owed that much to his brother.

***

12:35 PM

"Rajan is weak," said Akhtar as he walked back home with his son from their prayer.

"We should attack them now. We can take the entire city," said Ajmal.

"Patience, Ajmal. One wrong move and the entire police force will be looking at us," said Akhtar.

"We can do it quick and clean. I can guarantee that," said Ajmal quickly.

"My dear son, I plan to step down in the next two months. I thought it would be longer but I am now confident in your abilities," said Akhtar.

"You want me to distance myself from this, don't you?" Ajmal asked, looking at his father knowingly. His father nodded and grinned.

"Every news channel is showing him as some kind of cinema villain. All the police need is a nudge," said Akhtar with a grin.

"Rajan loves his brother. He won't allow this," said Ajmal. He saw his father's grin widen. "The minister," he said and smiled as he understood why his father was grinning.

***

4:30 PM

Minister Sharad Thakur was not in a good mood. He had just gotten an earful from the chief minister. There was a lot of public outrage after the video of Baaji went viral. The opposition was milking the issue, claiming failure of law and order. They had linked Rajan to the party and that irked many people.

Seniors from the party wanted to distance themselves from Rajan but the party needed Rajan. He could move around a lot of money and arrange manpower on short notice like no other. The chief minister wanted Baaji in jail and Rajan to publicly endorse the warrant. Sharad Thakur knew that this was not going to be easy.

Rajan would not give up his brother. He loved him far too much. He could not be tempted by money or power to betray his own blood. Despite being a gangster, Rajan was not someone who compromised on his own morals. He valued family more than anything. The minister knew this but the chief minister did not care.

The chief minister wanted this done and he did not care how. Sharad Thakur had been asked to be at a press conference along with Rajan to publicly announce the warrant. This was going to be close to impossible. Rajan arrived fifteen minutes after he had called him. He looked serious.

"How are you, Rajan?" the minister asked.

"My brother's son was killed, my brother is in hiding and I am a suspect. You tell me," said Rajan calmly.

"They suspect you? Are they right?" the minister asked.

Rajan looked hurt on hearing the question. "Gabbar was a troublesome kid but he was still a son to me. The DSP was lucky I did not smack him," said Rajan.

"What are you doing about Baaji?" the minister asked kindly.

"I have caused you a lot of trouble, haven't I?" Rajan asked.

"Nonsense. There is a way out of everything. In fact, I have a way to come out of this stronger. Enough about me. What are you doing about Baaji?" the minister asked.

"My lawyer says there is no way out of this. I can smuggle him to a different country and wait for this to cool down," said Rajan. He was careful not to mention how or where. He trusted the minister enough to tell him this much but not enough to give him details.

"May I suggest an alternative?" the minister asked.

"I am not letting you take my brother. I want him alive," said Rajan dismissively.

"He will be alive. Listen to me. Everyone knows that he is your brother. There is only one way to come out of this without spoiling your political future. Come with me to a press conference and announce that your brother will surrender. The jail is yours. You have so many of your men there. Baaji will be comfortable. The media will lose interest. As they do that, we can find legal loopholes to get him out," said the minister.

"I cannot see my brother behind bars," said Rajan dismissively.

"Be reasonable," said the minister.

"I am. This is my brother. I will give up anything

for him just like he would for me," said Rajan.

"Your love for each other is admirable. Think about this. You don't want to see him behind bars. The alternative is that you do not see him at all. The longer we delay this, the worse it will become for him. You can keep him comfortable in jail. We can arrange anything he desires in the prison," said the minister.

"No," said Rajan firmly.

"Don't be foolish, Rajan. Your brother was stupid enough to murder people in front of a camera. Don't be stupid enough to get him a death warrant," said the minister sharply. Rajan froze when he heard the word 'death warrant'. As much as he wanted his brother free, he wanted him alive. The minister was making sense.

Baaji got himself into this mess. This was the best chance Rajan had at keeping him alive. Sensing the change in Rajan's expression, the minister continued, "Tell your brother to surrender. We can keep him comfortable. We will gain a lot of political mileage from this."

"I don't care about political mileage but if this will keep Baaji alive, I will do anything you say," said Rajan.

A few minutes after Rajan left, the minister got a phone call. He did not have to answer it to guess who was calling.

"Akhtar Bhai, I haven't heard from you in years," said the minister warmly but he hated the old man. Akhtar did not treat him with the same respect that

Rajan gave him. He was full of wisecracks and full of himself.

"Yes. You have been involved with Rajan. I knew to stay out of it," said Akhtar.

"Working with Rajan has its advantages," said the minister. He had no interest in speaking to Akhtar but it would not hurt to hear him out.

"Thakur Sahab, it is finally time for us to work together," said Akhtar.

"How did you come to that conclusion?" the minister asked.

"Baaji is going down after this stunt on the news. He had half a brain and he proved it by killing in front of the cameras. He is going down and he was Rajan's muscle. We both know that," said Akhtar.

"What do you propose?" the minister asked.

"Have him encountered. The people will love you for it and nobody will lose sleep over it. Once I wipe out Rajan, you will have a better ally in me," said Akhtar.

"I don't have the habit of stabbing my people in the back. Thanks, but no thanks, Akhtar Bhai," said the minister sharply. As confident as Akhtar was in his abilities, he had no idea how strong Rajan really was. Rajan was as violent as Baaji but he knew how to maintain an image. His cleverness made him more dangerous.

The minister decided to end the conversation quickly. Having Baaji encountered had crossed his mind but he had reached a much better solution with Rajan. This was one that would keep everyone happy. He would get the credit, Rajan would get a posting, Baaji would get to keep his life and the city would not suffer major violence again.

Akhtar was surprised. The minister had been an opportunist all his life but he had flatly refused him. "Fool," he said, feeling disappointed.

"Don't worry," said Ajmal with a grin.

"What do you have in mind?" Akhtar asked.

"There is more than one way to get what we want," said Ajmal as he took his phone and looked for a specific contact. Akhtar looked at his son doubtfully. "Relax, this can never be traced back to us," added Ajmal knowingly.

Akhtar looked at his son and smiled. Ajmal was smart. He wondered if Ajmal had been too smart and had orchestrated Gabbar's murder behind his back. He had the brains for it. Akhtar sat next to Ajmal as Shaheena entered the room. They became silent. The only sound in the room was the sound from the old fan.

"Did you have anything to do with Gabbar's murder?" Akhtar asked slowly. Shaheena looked surprised but said nothing.

Ajmal smiled. "You are my father," he said politely.

"That doesn't answer my question," said Akhtar sharply.

"You have decided to give the business to me. You should start trusting my decision making. If you don't, then you have made the wrong choice. I don't think my father makes wrong choices," said Ajmal softly.

Akhtar looked surprised by the answer. He wanted to say something but he realised that he did not have a good comeback. He smiled weakly and left the room. Once he was out of earshot, Shaheena cleared her throat. "You could have told him the truth," she said seriously.

"I know," said Ajmal with a serious look on his face. His father was getting old and Ajmal wasn't getting any younger. His father was talking about handing over the business to him. That meant that he had to live with Ajmal's decisions.

***

8:30 PM

Four hours later, Rajan was in a press conference with the law minister, the IG and a few other police personnel. The minister had given him a few lines to memorise in case he was questioned. He had sent word to Baaji to surrender quietly. Baaji did not like it but he agreed when Manish explained the situation to him and told him that it was the only way.

Rajan was to announce the warrant without saying anything about the actual incident. He was supposed to say that justice would be served and that being his family did not absolve his brother. The minister would question the authenticity of the video pointedly while standing by Rajan. Rajan remained calm and tried not to frown. He kept looking around aimlessly while trying to keep a straight face. As he kept staring, the minister nudged him.

He walked to the dais a few feet away and spoke softly, "Nobody is above the law. I do not know if my brother did what you say he did but he is not above the law. I have personally requested a warrant for the arrest of my brother and we expect him to surrender in the next twenty-four hours. If found guilty, he will be prosecuted per the law."

"Are you trying to tell us that your brother is innocent? We have him committing murder on tape," said one of the reporters in the front row.

Rajan clicked his tongue and stared at the reporter. He then smiled weakly, pointed to the warrant and walked back to his seat without answering the question.

"The most important thing here is that the police will arrest Baaji in the next twenty-four hours. Our party believes in the law and the legal system. If we find him guilty, he will be punished," said the minister, taking over the dais.

Rajan kept forcing that smile but it was becoming increasingly difficult. He wanted to smash something. The reporters were irritating. They were looking for an admission of guilt but the minister was an expert at this. He was talking about justice, law and governance and the reporters were lapping it up. Rajan did not blame Thakur. This was the only way. Baaji had been stupid.

One by one, the reporters left. The others also left until only Rajan was left in the room. The minister placed a consoling arm on his shoulder and said, "This is for the best."

"I know it is but it doesn't feel good," said Rajan.

CHAPTER 11

AN INCONVENIENT SHOOTOUT

The riot squad was called to bring Baaji in quietly. Baaji had called the IG in a conference call with the law minister and his brother to convey his intention to surrender. With half the city looking for him, the police did not feel that it was safe to travel all the way to the court to surrender. Baaji was holed up in a property owned by him in the outskirts of the city. He had told them that he would surrender to them unconditionally in that location.

Gaurav knew that everything would stop with his surrender and he could go back to his old job. His children had a few days of their vacation left. He could leave that night itself. He was not completely convinced with how the case had unfolded but he decided not to delve into it. His life was more important than this case and he was going to achieve what he was called for. The city would return to normalcy once again.

***

9:45 PM

"You aren't coming?" the DCP asked.

"He is going to surrender. It is a long drive," said Gaurav uneasily.

"You can go back to your governor later. Come on. Let's celebrate. We are ending this nightmare today. We are closing everything related to Gabbar's murder," said the DCP.

Gaurav looked at the DCP doubtfully. While they had closed the case with Hemant as the killer, he felt there was something missing. He knew that Cyrus could not have arranged it. If someone had turned Hemant against Gabbar, it would have been Akhtar. It made no sense for Baaji to go after. He had expected Baaji to be smarter but the loss of his son had taken away his ability to think properly.

He had ended his criminal career in the process. Gaurav could not believe that Hemant could have killed Gabbar. Being that close to Gabbar all the time, someone would have noticed something. The fact that Hemant died and Angel was not harmed only reaffirmed his doubt. Angel had not just been unharmed. She had been living in Rajan's house since then.

"It is a surrender. It will be boring," said Gaurav reluctantly.

"It is the most action you are going to see in a really long time. Once you go back to the governor's office, you will be chasing crows on his terrace," said the DCP snidely.

"How do you know that?" Gaurav asked, feeling embarrassed.

"You think I would not keep track of you?" the DCP asked playfully. "Come on. One last time. Let's watch Baaji surrender. Who knows? We might not see such an event for the rest of our careers."

Gaurav rode with the DCP and Krishna in the car towards the outskirts where Baaji was hiding. It was a long drive during which they reminisced about their time working together. He kept his hand on his face. Hemant's kick to his face did not leave any mark luckily but it still hurt.

"Now that this case is over, do you want to leave the governor's office for this?" Krishna asked casually.

"He has interesting chases there on a daily basis. He won't be missing much," said the DCP sharply before Gaurav could open his mouth.

"I didn't know it was exciting there. I must ask for a transfer," said Krishna innocently.

"Sure. I will be happy to have you," said Gaurav calmly.

"Stop poaching my assets. Krishna is going to be with us and deal with the boring stuff. Maybe after I retire," said the DCP with a grin.

"You were not joking, were you? I haven't seen anything in the news about chases by the governor's staff," said Krishna innocently.

"It is top secret, Krishna ji," said the DCP.

"Is he making fun of you?" Krishna asked with a grin.

"Please drive, Krishna ji. He is going to have all his fun today," said Gaurav, grinning awkwardly. He winced as his face hurt due to the grin.

***

10:40 PM

When they reached the spot, the riot squad had already assembled. A dozen of them were in formation but there were others around the area. Gaurav felt like a hero when the entire group saluted him. He then realised that the salute was for the DCP, who did not make much of an effort to hide his laughter.

"What is the situation?" the DCP asked, becoming serious and beckoning Gaurav.

"Baaji is in that building. He has three people with him. We have cleared the area and we have thirty men around the area," said a riot policeman.

"Civilians?" the DCP asked.

"We have pulled everyone off the street and a few from the surrounding streets as well. Nobody suspicious," he replied.

"Alright. I want this done quickly and cleanly. I want him taken into custody and the van moving within fifteen minutes," said the DCP.

Gaurav and the DCP sat in the car, listening to

their wireless as the riot squad closed in on the building. The squad leader was reporting every few seconds. Things were going as per plan but Gaurav had a bad feeling. Things were too silent for his liking. They sat looking at the wireless as though it was giving them the commentary for the last over of the World Cup final. Just as they sat looking at the wireless, they heard a sound that broke the silence.

"Was that?" Gaurav asked doubtfully, not wanting to say the word.

The DCP raised his hand. Then they heard it again and the DCP swore.

"Shots fired," came the voice on the wireless.

"Which one of you complete idiots got too excited with your trigger finger?" the DCP shouted.

"It wasn't one of us," said the voice on the wireless.

"Baaji has guns here?" the DCP asked doubtfully, muting his line. There were a number of shots heard at very short intervals after that. The DCP banged his hand on the car door and swore again. "Someone tell me what the hell is happening there," shouted the DCP at his walkie.

"They have opened fire. We are taking cover," said the voice on the wireless.

"Get the minister on the phone," said the DCP to Gaurav urgently.

"This is law minister, Sharad Thakur. I am hearing bullets. What are you jokers doing?" the minister asked.

They looked at each other in shock. The minister was nearby and speaking via the wireless.

"How did he get here?" the DCP asked as he muted their line.

"He must only be a short distance away," said Gaurav, looking around. The wireless had a very short range. He looked out but he was not sure where the minister was.

"Sir, we are facing heavy gunfire. Multiple men with guns are firing at us," said the man from the wireless.

"Sir, do we have permission to fire?" the DCP asked, unsure of himself. The line was silent. "Sir? We could lose our men if we don't retaliate," he added after a minute. The DCP shook his head as they heard more bullets.

"You have my permission to fire. Do not kill him. That would destroy this city," the minister finally said when the DCP was at the edge of his patience.

Anyone who did not know what was happening would have thought that there was a festival in the area. The gunshots were continuous, like crackers. After fourteen minutes of intermittent firing, the area went silent.

"We have them. One of the shooters is dead but we have Baaji alive. We need medical assistance," said a voice on the wireless.

"Is Baaji hurt?" the minister asked but there was no answer.

There was a lot of noise but they could comprehend nothing. "Someone tell me what is going on," shouted the DCP. As he spoke, he could hear the ambulance. "This is bad," said the DCP, exiting the car. Gaurav followed him. All the policemen had gathered at one spot. The minister was nowhere to be seen.

The riot policeman who had been speaking to them on the wireless came running towards them. He had blood on his neck and his uniform.

"Are you hurt?" the DCP asked, looking worried.

"This is not my blood," said the man.

"How bad is Baaji? Is he shot?" the DCP asked.

"He was shot by—" began the policeman nervously.

"I don't want to know. Tell nobody. Tell your team to never speak of this. Whoever has blood on them, stay away from the minister's eyes. Trust nobody because this is Baaji," said the DCP in a hushed tone.

"We had no choice. They were firing and hit—" began the man awkwardly.

"It doesn't matter. It is over. Now take this to your grave. If not, Rajan will put you in one," said the DCP. He patted the man on the shoulder. "How is Baaji?" he asked kindly.

"He will live," said the man quietly.

"That is all that matters. Walk away now. You can brief me later," said the DCP.

The minister arrived not long after. Gaurav and the DCP assured him that Baaji was put in an ambulance. He had been in a van nearby with his own set of guards. Rajan was with him and he looked furious.

The minister took the DCP aside. "Is he alive, Patel?" he asked the DCP.

"He will live. It is a flesh wound but we don't know the extent of the damage yet. One of his men is dead," said the DCP.

"I don't care about any of his men. What about our men? Are any policemen hurt?" the minister asked.

"One, but it is not a bullet wound. Any idea why they fired?" the DCP said.

"I don't know which idiot from their gang started it but Rajan is going to give him hell for it," said the minister, walking away.

"What a day!" the DCP said as he sat in the car.

"Baaji is going to jail. That is a win," said Gaurav.

"Gabbar was killed by Hemant. Hemant was hired by Cyrus. Baaji killed Cyrus and now, Baaji is going to jail for a long time," said the DCP.

"Baaji killed Cyrus but that is the only thing we know for a fact," said Gaurav.

"Listen to me carefully. This case is closed. Do not even attempt to create any doubts around this. Everybody is happy and you know how much of a pipe dream that was a few days ago. The case is closed. You can do the paperwork if you can be silent or else, I will have the sub-inspector do it. Go back to your governor," said the DCP.

"Gun Baba did not—" began Gaurav earnestly.

"I don't care if Sai Baba said it. The case is closed. Even Rajan is convinced. Do not stir anything. You will go back and I will be left with the mess," said the DCP.

"But," began Gaurav in protest.

"This is not like one of those movies where the hero is a policeman who has great instincts. Your skill is negotiating for peace. That happened. Do not try to do anything else," said the DCP, looking at Gaurav with a worried expression.

"The case is not closed. We have no proof," said Gaurav.

"I like you, Gaurav, but I got you on this case to avoid a war. You did that for me but this is the end of the line for you. Go back and chase your crows. Please!" the DCP said.

Gaurav remained silent. He was not convinced with the way the case had been closed. Hemant did not strike him as a killer. He neither had reason nor the means to do this. If he did, he would not have been in the same area while they were searching for him. That was extremely stupid. Cyrus was getting strong but he did not have the courage to organise something like this. It just did not feel right.

"I have a theory and you are not going to like it," said Gaurav. He had investigated a lot of angles and he had more questions now than when the case began.

"I don't want any more theories. I only want a

smooth trial," said the DCP.

"I am serious. I don't think Hemant did this," said Gaurav.

The DCP shushed him and worked on finishing the formalities at the scene. Looking at Gaurav's disappointed look, he asked him to wait until they were back at his office. It was three hours later when they began to discuss the matter.

***

1:30 AM

"I think we have been looking at it all wrong," said Gaurav as he began to explain his theory an hour later. "Gabbar died early in the morning. The murder itself was suspicious. Gabbar was never alone, no matter where he went. Even when he was with his mistress, he had his men waiting outside. Blade and Hemant were like his shadows. They never left him."

"So? They were held for being drunk that night, weren't they?" the DCP asked.

"Hemant was held and I think it was intended to be that way. The killer wanted to isolate him from his friends. There was a barricade in their usual route. The barricade, according to one of his men, was not easy to move. They had the habit of moving barricades in their area whenever they wanted. This was difficult. That is why they chose the other route.

"At this point, Blade was missing already. He was supposed to be out of town but he was actually dead at the time. They were not aware of it. He was killed in the marina area. That is not easy to do without people noticing. There are people who saw him chase a woman clad in white," said Gaurav, drawing a map of the area.

"What are you implying?" the DCP asked.

"Whoever did this, knew this area. They knew it in and out. Isolating Gabbar and killing him where nobody would hear the fight requires a lot of knowledge of the area. I don't know if Gabbar injured his killer. We found more than fifty different DNA samples within a two feet radius. The whole area was a cesspool of DNA. Whoever this person was, he had intimate knowledge of the marina area and Gabbar's gang," said Gaurav.

"You are sure that this is a man?" the DCP asked.

"Not necessarily. A right-handed person, more likely a man. Those injuries to Gabbar were made by a strong person. Blade and Gabbar were killed by the same person. The injuries are consistent. Whoever this was, they knew how to isolate them and finish them off one by one. Both these men were good fighters. He was either able to overpower them or he took them by surprise," said Gaurav.

"Who did it?" the DCP asked, scratching his bald head.

"Someone from the department or close to it," said Gaurav confidently.

"Why? How?" the DCP asked, looking surprised.

"Nobody from that gang has the guts to strike down Gabbar. Hemant is a forced fit but I am sure that he could not have done this. His death proved that," said Gaurav.

"What do you mean?" the DCP asked.

"Hemant was killed. I don't know by whom but he did not fall from that building by accident. I'm certain that their orders were to catch him but since we were very close to catching him, they killed him," said Gaurav.

"You cannot be serious. How does this lead to someone in our department?" the DCP asked incredulously.

"Hemant's death looked natural. He fell off the building but I have seen enough people fall from buildings in my life. He did not slip. He jumped or he was pushed. Look at the photos. The angle and the projectile will back my claim. We cannot prove that in court but this is one of those things that we know by experience.

"There was a cell phone with him, which I remember from the scene. That phone was missing when the evidence was tagged. Tampering with evidence needs a really smart person," said Gaurav.

"Are you sure?" the DCP asked.

"I would not be telling you all this if I was not sure," said Gaurav.

"Go on," said the DCP, leaning back in his chair.

"This is where things escalated. Someone knew that Baaji was going to take Cyrus out. The video sent to the news channels was from a traffic camera. Someone had turned the camera to make sure that it captured the events in the market. I checked with the IT guys. That was our camera. I did not give that to the press for obvious reasons. They say that there is no evidence of anyone hacking our system," said Gaurav.

"One of our IT guys did this?" the DCP asked.

"Not necessarily. It was done by someone who had access to our systems. It would have taken a fit individual to handle someone like Gabbar and we don't have such people in our IT department. That leaves someone on active duty. In addition to that, the murder looks personal. I am fairly certain that someone who works this area did this," said Gaurav.

"This is a catastrophe," said the DCP.

"I have more," said Gaurav.

"It doesn't matter," said the DCP.

"Oh. Then I have a question," said Gaurav.

"What?" the DCP asked.

"Was this an encounter operation?" Gaurav asked.

"Don't be stupid," said the DCP dismissively.

"There was no task-force, there was no special investigation squad and a lot of it seems suspicious," said Gaurav doubtfully.

"First of all, this is real life. Police do not do

encounters. It is illegal. Don't ever talk like this with anyone again. There was no special investigation? Why do you think I got you here? Do you have any idea about the kind of pressure that I have been in? I know the case is fishy but don't go making ridiculous claims about the department," said the DCP.

"I might be off in the encounter angle but I know that Hemant did not kill Gabbar. We are being forced to close this case," said Gaurav.

"You think that the department is involved because we want to close the case? Are you mad, Gaurav?" the DCP asked.

"That is just a possibility. I don't know. Perhaps, I am overthinking stuff," said Gaurav.

"Sometimes, you have to accept that you won. Don't question your gifts. Go on to your vacation. I'll have Siddique do the paperwork. You can review it later. Leave now. I don't want you looking at further angles or discussing this with anyone else. This case is done. I cannot have you opening a can of worms now. I don't know about your claims on the case but we have reached an end to the violence and that is more important to me than anything else," said the DCP, kindly placing his hand on Gaurav's shoulder.

Gaurav realised that he had one more thing left to do before he ended his involvement in this case. He drove to Rajan's house alone. A lot of people would say that he was being stupid but he knew Rajan very well. Rajan was one of the smartest people in his line of work. He knew how to balance emotion and logic. When they met, Rajan was surprised to see him.

"You have the nerve to come here alone?" Rajan asked as he looked down at Gaurav from his terrace. He did not look pleased.

"We need to talk, Rajan. I am not here as a policeman," said Gaurav, looking Rajan in the eye. He wanted to convey his thoughts to Rajan but he did not want to make him angry.

Rajan did not speak a word as Gaurav told him what he had on his mind. The DCP was happy to have avoided a war but he wanted to avoid the cold war that would follow it. If the cold war was not avoided, violence could break out at any time. Rajan did not react and ordered him to leave as soon as he had said his piece. Gaurav was not sure whether he had made his point but he was glad that he got it off his chest.

With a heavy heart, Gaurav boarded the bus. He was taking his delayed vacation but he did not feel that he had finished his work. He was going to meet his kids after weeks and be away from work but he kept thinking about the case. He called his wife and told her that he was coming. She was overjoyed.

One thing kept bugging him as he closed his eyes and leaned back in his seat. He had a feeling that they had the wrong person. He was usually right about these things. It did not fit. He kept going through the case in his mind. Nothing made sense. Gabbar and his men died. Hemant was their best suspect but he suspiciously fell off a building and died.

The DCP wanted the case closed at that point despite nobody being convinced that Hemant had masterminded this. Hemant did not fit the profile of the killer but given the sensitive nature of the case, everyone wanted it to fit. They wanted the case closed as soon as possible.

Gaurav had been investigating further when the incident with Baaji happened. Baaji had murdered Cyrus and his gang in cold blood. The most surprising part of that was that someone had recorded the entire incident. They had also delivered it to several media houses. Gaurav had followed up on the packages but the packages had been physically delivered.

Nobody remembered who had delivered the package and there was nothing recorded by the cameras. Gaurav had found that the camera was a police traffic camera. Somehow, it had been at the right position at that time. He had no idea how the video was taken from the servers and shared outside. Something did not fit. The systems were not secure but it was not that easy to hack them. That had created a lot of doubt in his mind.

The most surprising event was Baaji's surrender. It was like a blessing when they received word that he was surrendering. Gaurav knew that he would never see something like this again in his life. Dons seldom surrendered like this. Shockingly, one of his men had opened fire at the police. That worsened the situation.

Baaji was shot, which made the bad situation worse. It did not make sense that someone like Baaji would carefully negotiate a surrender without keeping his men informed and under control. The whole shooting was suspicious. While it was not fatal, the doctors expected the injury to restrict his mobility temporarily. They were still waiting for the details on the extent of the damage. Gaurav raised concerns that the firing was suspicious but the DCP wanted the case closed.

There were too many loose ends but Gaurav knew that it was not his problem anymore. He had handed the paperwork to Siddique and he was to return to the governor's detail after his vacation. He only needed to review the paperwork and sign it later. Despite the unexpected ending to the case, the DCP was happy with him.

They were now at better terms than before. When he woke up the next morning, his wife was waiting at the bus stop. She had driven the scooter early in the morning to pick him up. It had been a long time since they saw each other. They took a long detour before reaching home. Absence really did make the heart grow fonder. They had missed each other. They did not realise how much until they met.

CHAPTER 12

OVERDUE VACATION

Gaurav was enjoying his vacation with his children. In the city, they seldom got the chance to do absolutely nothing. The entire family went to the river near the house in the evenings. The area was secluded but safe. He often went on walks with Sunitha by the riverside. They had their own favourite spot, which overlooked the river.

It was the best spot in the entire stretch. Gaurav lay on the soft sand with his head on his wife's lap. His father-in-law was watching his children swim. They had become very good at it. His mother-in-law was standing by the river with towels in her hand and a look of concern on her face.

"Ma, let them be in the water for a little longer. They won't see water like this until the next vacation," shouted Sunitha.

"It has been more than an hour. This is enough. You better stop screaming. You are disturbing your husband's nap," said Sunitha's mother.

"It's cute that she thinks that I am asleep," said Gaurav, grinning with his eyes closed.

"You are finally here. That's good. My mother thinks you are Mahatma Gandhi. You can do no wrong in her eyes," said Sunitha, gently untwirling his moustache.

"That makes you angry?" Gaurav asked playfully.

"She can think I am not the devil at least," said Sunitha, looking grumpy.

"Stop being grumpy. We are going home tomorrow and you will miss her almost immediately," said Gaurav, reaching for his moustache.

"That is how mothers and daughters are. Ignore it," she said, grinning. She kept staring at her kids fondly for a few minutes and then turned back to him. "Are you not having fun here? You don't seem to be yourself this time," said Sunitha, smacking his hand away.

"I am having fun. Don't be stupid," said Gaurav playfully.

"Is it about the case? I saw the news every day after you told me. It must have been bad," she said.

"It was bad but not for me. It is over now but I just feel like I did not close it properly," said Gaurav thoughtfully.

"What do you mean? You arrested Rajan's brother in the end. What more do you want?" Sunitha asked.

"We closed the case but I didn't solve it," said Gaurav.

"I was worried when you told me that you were

going back to your old department," said Sunitha, looking worried.

"Don't worry. I just need to sign the paperwork when the SI from the station finishes it and then I am back to being the governor's watchman," said Gaurav, kissing her hand reassuringly.

"I don't like you going back to that department. We have a good thing here. Let us not ruin it," said Sunitha, looking concerned.

"I didn't have a choice this time. I won't go back, no matter what happens. It may seem like I don't enjoy it but I like what we have now too. I will try to stay here until I retire," said Gaurav reassuringly. He held her hand and looked into her eyes. "I will be safe. I know how to stay out of trouble."

"I know that. That is not what I am afraid of," said Sunitha.

"What do you mean?" Gaurav asked.

"You get too involved in these cases. You don't notice it but you begin to forget everything due to your involvement," said Sunitha.

Gaurav did not know if this was true but he knew that Sunitha genuinely felt this way. He wondered if his change in role had effects that went beyond material satisfaction. He realised that he may have misunderstood his wife. He held her hand and looked at his kids. His mind raced back to the case.

He could not understand what he had

missed. Perhaps his wife was right. He got too immersed in his cases. He brushed the thoughts off his mind. He had one more week of his vacation left. He wanted to make the most of it.

***

6:40 PM (TWO WEEKS AFTER BAAJI'S SURRENDER)

Ajmal was walking with his father after their evening prayers. He had been waiting to talk to him about recent events but they never discussed business in the mosque. The evening prayer was special to both of them. While they did their other prayers on their own wherever they were, they always did their evening prayer together in the mosque. Ajmal waited patiently until they were alone to discuss business.

"Baaji is alive," said Ajmal sombrely.

"I heard. That is a setback," said Akhtar quietly. He was disappointed. He hesitated for a moment and then shook his head. He closed his eyes and sighed heavily before turning to face Ajmal. "Our man," he began nervously.

"Dead. He didn't say a word. I am almost sure of it," said Ajmal.

"Almost?" Akhtar asked, looking surprised.

Ajmal remained quiet. There was no way to be certain. Baaji was still alive though his man was dead.

He hoped that Baaji had not found out that it was their man who had opened fire at the police to force their hand. Even with Baaji in the hospital, Rajan was a formidable enemy. They were the biggest powers in the city and a war would weaken both of them considerably. If Rajan knew this, he would stop at nothing.

"We need to be ready," said Akhtar solemnly. He knew that this could not stay hidden for long. As they stood talking, they heard footsteps. They both turned to see a woman walking towards them. Ajmal squinted to see who it was but Akhtar froze.

"How are you doing, brother? You have grown into a handsome man, Ajmal," said Nasreen calmly. Ajmal was stunned to see his aunt but Akhtar was angry. He turned away as he did not want to look at her.

"How did you get here?" Ajmal asked.

"I grew up here. I know this place better than you," said Nasreen with a grin. She was clad in a pale blue hijab and a matching dress. Anyone there could mistake her for a woman who had come for prayers. "Will you not talk to me, brother?" she asked politely.

"You are no sister of mine. I do not wish to see you," said Akhtar scathingly.

"What did I do wrong that you won't even look at my face?" Nasreen asked, looking visibly hurt.

"Ajmal! Tell her to leave or I will kill her at this very spot," said the old man angrily.

Ajmal looked uncomfortable. He had no love for

Nasreen and did not care that she was his aunt. Rajan was his enemy and she was his wife. Any memory that he had of her before she married Rajan was ignored. He would not hesitate to kill her. Nasreen looked torn but she stood her ground.

"Get out of my sight!" Akhtar shouted menacingly. He stepped forward aggressively with his hand raised.

Nasreen did not flinch. She stepped forward and turned her face to show him her cheek. "Go on! I will not stop you," said Nasreen boldly. Akhtar stopped in his tracks. "You have been wanting to kill me for years. I am here. Kill me now," she said, screaming at him.

Ajmal looked around to make sure that there was nobody else. Her screams pierced the silence of the empty alleyway. "Go away before we hurt you," he said, warning her.

"You want me to go now? I understand why he is mad at me. Why are you? You used to be on my shoulders every minute that you were awake. Did you forget all that?" Nasreen asked, looking pained.

"He was not just a brother to you. He raised you like a father would have. You left him for Rajan. You had to marry someone who is not one of us. You betrayed him. You are dead to all of us," said Ajmal sharply.

"Go ahead then. Kill me. Come on. You two have been trying it for so long. Let us finish this tonight. My husband will die the moment he hears I am dead. That should be a double delight for the both of you.

Go on. You raised me, brother. Kill me!" Nasreen said, stepping forward towards Akhtar.

Ajmal saw his father do something he did not expect. He stepped back. He looked at her calmly but Ajmal could see that his father was clueless. This was unexpected.

"Go ahead, brother. You have claimed that you would make me a widow, kill me with your own hands, kill my children and so much more. I have heard it all. Finish me here and get it over with. This is the one promise that the great Akhtar Bhai has not been able to keep. Kill me now, brother," she said, walking closer to him.

"Nasreen Bua, step back or I will—" began Ajmal angrily.

"Took you long enough to address me correctly. Your father doesn't seem to be able to kill me. Why don't you?" she asked sternly. "Speak to me. Is all this because I married someone outside our community?" she asked menacingly, turning to her brother.

"He is a criminal. A killer!" Akhtar said, breaking his silence.

"What about you? What about him? Don't tell me that you are saints. We are all criminals. We are all bad people. You have killed. He has killed. I have been a mute spectator and so, I am culpable in all your crimes. Your problem has been that I married an outsider," said Nasreen scathingly.

"You married my enemy," shouted Akhtar.

"So what? He loves me despite the fact that you are his enemy. You could never have found someone for me who treats me the way he does. You? You stopped loving me because I loved him. I still love my brother and he doesn't love me any less for it. He is a far better man than you will ever be," said Nasreen and broke down into tears. "My own brother wanted to kill me. My own brother wanted my kids—" she said, breaking down finally.

"I am sorry," said Akhtar. He did not want her to complete her last sentence. Every word that she had spoken hit him like a bullet. He had been angry with the wrong person. Nasreen had been everything to him and he had lost her. Ajmal looked surprised but remained a mute spectator.

Nasreen stood a few feet away, crying in a low voice. They heard footsteps again and turned to look behind her. Rajan was walking calmly. Ajmal realised that he had no weapons. He looked around and saw a broken pipe near the wall. He reached for it when he heard Rajan's deep voice.

"If I wanted to kill you, you would be dead. I came here empty-handed. I just want to talk," said Rajan calmly. He walked forward, unmindful of his enemies. Nasreen leaned over his shoulder and dried her eyes on his sleeve. "Akhtar Bhai, you and I will never be anything but enemies. We both know that. I told

Nasreen that you would hate her if she married me. She foolishly believed that you would be able to look past my religion," said Rajan calmly.

Akhtar was not emotional anymore. He stared at Rajan and looked like he was ready to kill him. Ajmal came to his side and was alert and ready, in case they had to fight. Rajan was more concerned about his wife.

"Why are you here? Are you trying to gain my mercy by having your wife beg?" Akhtar asked rudely. He wanted to provoke Rajan and belittle him.

"My wife told me that her brother would change if he saw her. I told her that she would be disappointed," said Rajan, kindly putting his arm over his wife's shoulder. "I came here to come to an agreement. My wife was foolish enough to believe that you would treat her as a human."

"Why are you here? Have you come to surrender?" Ajmal asked.

"Ajmal, I have nothing against you. Your father will hand over his business to you soon. What you are to your father, Gabbar was to me. I lost him," said Rajan calmly. Nasreen had composed herself and stood firmly next to her husband.

"We don't care if you were involved in Gabbar's murder. You don't need to bother accepting or denying it," said Nasreen sharply.

"We live with violence but no amount of violence can prepare us for the loss of loved ones. I lost Gabbar and I know that you almost made me lose Baaji. I cannot lose my brother too. That is why I am here. I do not want any attempts on his life," said Rajan. Akhtar was calm but Ajmal was stunned. That gave it away.

"Have you come here for mercy?" Akhtar asked coyly.

"Do not mistake my husband's presence here for weakness. We are in the heart of your area and none of your men even noticed it. I am the only one holding him back. I will for as long as I live but do not test that limit," said Nasreen menacingly.

Ajmal looked surprised. He remembered very little of his aunt from all those years ago. This was a threat, delivered exactly like his father would have. The tone, the stance and even the wording was similar. She really was his sister.

"What do you want, Rajan?" Akhtar asked.

"You and me, we can never be anything but enemies. Akhtar Bhai, we are different people. The only thing common between us is that we both keep our word. Stay out of my business and I will do the same for you. I have lost a boy who was like a son to me. I will let that go but I will not watch my brother get hurt. If he gets so much as a scratch, you will know what I am truly capable of," said Rajan. Ajmal noticed that he was polite and respectful despite making a threat.

Akhtar stared at Rajan for a long time. Ajmal kept looking at his father and then realised it. His father was a practical man. He knew that a war with Rajan would damage everyone. They would also get unnecessary attention from the police. His father turned to him and nodded. He knew that his father expected him to make the statement. He was projecting him to Rajan as the next leader. Ajmal stood erect and turned to Rajan.

"This city is big enough for the both of us. You make a good proposition. We will let you know our decision soon," said Ajmal confidently.

Rajan looked at Ajmal. He knew that the decision had been made. He wanted to give them a parting shot. "You can send word through your spy in my gang. What is his name? Bantu?" Rajan asked with a grin and turned to walk away.

Ajmal hid his surprise. Akhtar was indifferent. "Nasreen!" Akhtar called. Nasreen looked surprised as she turned to him. She turned to look at her brother who had called her by name after several years. His voice was almost kind. "You must know that I would never hurt you. Whatever I may have said was not from the heart. I have wanted to kill Rajan for taking you away from me. There is no denying that, but I would never harm you or your children. I never meant to do that, and I will not for as long as I live," he said reassuringly. The proud old don turned away, not wanting his rival to see him tear up.

Rajan waited for a moment. Ajmal came forward and held Nasreen's hand. Rajan stepped away to let them have a moment to compose themselves. Unlike his father, Ajmal was not emotional. He was calm but smiled weakly. He determinedly stared away from Rajan. He nodded at Nasreen and then walked back to his father. Rajan placed his arm on Nasreen's shoulder and turned to leave.

"This doesn't change anything between us," said Akhtar as Rajan walked away.

"I don't expect it to," said Rajan as he disappeared from sight.

***

10:30 AM (THE NEXT DAY)

"Gaurav," called a familiar voice and Gaurav turned to see the DCP.

"Good afternoon, Sir," said Gaurav, giving the DCP a customary salute.

"I thought you would be back chasing crows now," he said jovially as he came closer.

"I thought so too but I have the paperwork to complete. I thought I would finish that at the earliest," said Gaurav.

"How was the vacation?" the DCP asked as they walked to his cabin.

"It was good. I am glad the case ended in time," said Gaurav.

"Speaking of ending, I am sorry I forced you to end

the case. I just could not afford to keep it open," said the DCP.

"I understand. It was not worth the scandal it would have created. It is better this way. I was glad I could help you," said Gaurav politely.

"I know. I will not forget this. You helped me in a time of need. I would ask you back to my department but I know that you are happy with the governor," said the DCP.

"I am. I am also happy to have helped you. I will review the paperwork and send it back to you soon," said Gaurav.

"Thank you," said the DCP, showing him out.

Gaurav went to collect the rest of the paperwork. As he did, he signed the register.

"Sir, that is the leave register," said the writer, handing him the correct register. Gaurav had his eyes fixed on the register. He was surprised and his mind began to race.

"Thank you. Can I take this with me?" he asked the writer politely.

"You want our leave register?" the writer asked.

"I will return it as soon as I can," said Gaurav.

"The DCP said that I must give you whatever you want. Make sure you return it soon. Now that this case is over, many people want to take leave," said the man politely.

Gaurav was not listening. His mind was racing. He

could understand why he was having sudden doubts about how the case was closed. He had an intuition on seeing the register. He wanted to check this. He had always doubted that someone in the department had done this. Looking at the register, he saw an entry that caught his attention again.

CHAPTER 13

THE CAUSAL INCIDENT

10:15 PM (SIX WEEKS AGO)

Jameela walked along the dimly lit road. She hated coming to this route but she was scared of the dogs that terrorised her in the usual route. She clutched her bag tightly as she walked the road. The road was dark, empty, scary and gave her nightmares. She wished she had called her brother. If he was with her, she would have felt safe.

She took her phone and dialled Nawaz instead. Her marriage had been fixed to Nawaz three months ago. His phone kept ringing but he wasn't picking up. Nawaz was a nurse in the government hospital. He kept his phone away when he was at work. She cursed softly as she put her phone into her bag. Something small and black moved close to her foot.

She froze immediately. She had her eyes tightly shut, too scared to even scream. After almost a minute, she looked down at her feet where she felt some movement. It looked as big as a cat but it was a huge rat running around her feet. Someone had spilled some food and it was nibbling away at it happily.

Her heart, which had been thundering against her ribs, came back to a steady pace as she caught her breath. She stepped away from the rat and walked forward. She was walking on a road close to the sea and was feeling cold. She wanted to take the shawl out of her bag but she did not want to waste any time on this path. She wanted to cross it as soon as possible.

She took a few steps forward and heard a few voices. That relaxed her a little bit but before she could take a breath, she panicked even more. It was the sound of a few men drinking and shouting. They were heavily drunk. She hastened her pace to get out of there but she stepped on an empty plastic bottle.

The sound of crushing the plastic cut through the silence of the night. Before she could take another step, the laughing stopped. As she looked around, the men had been alerted and were staring in her direction. In a flash, they surrounded her. There were three men there. She did not know two of them but the third one was Gabbar. He was Baaji's son and the most feared person in the area.

"Who are you?" one of the men asked.

"It doesn't matter. Walk away, girl!" the second man barked rudely.

Throwing away the chicken bone he had had in his hand, Gabbar began to lick his fingers. He had been more interested in the chicken than Jameela so far. As he continued to lick his fingers, he took a good look at her. That look creeped her out. One of the men shook his head and turned away.

The other man looked at Gabbar with a conflicted look. Gabbar towered over them. He was tall and looked dangerous. Before he could speak, Gabbar slapped him and turned his head away. Both men stepped away but were within earshot.

Gabbar came close to her. He looked like an animal closing in on a terrified prey. "If you do as I say, you will not be harmed. This will be over quickly and you can go," he said softly as he began to drool. One of the men poured water from a bottle as he washed his hands. He splashed a little water on his face and grabbed the bottle. He gargled a little bit of water and spat, aiming between Jameela's legs. It was the most disgusting sight in her entire life. Gabbar was advancing towards her and she could not move her limbs.

"Please," she said with folded hands, stepping back.

"Stop moving," he barked. That sent another chill down her spine. This time she froze. "Spend some time with me. I will give you a lot of money," he said, pulling out a fat wad of cash and waving it at her face.

"Please, brother! I am not that kind of girl. Please let me go. I just want to go home," she said tearfully. She began to look around to see if she could make a run for it but Gabbar's men would catch her easily.

"Don't call me brother," said Gabbar loudly. He shook his head after saying the word.

"Please. Let me go," said Jameela but he grabbed her by the neck and dragged her to where they were drinking and pinned her to the ground. As she began to choke, he let go of her neck and pressed her shoulder. He was heavy and easily incapacitated her. She struggled hard, trying to release herself, but froze completely when he took out a knife.

"If you even try to hit me, I will make sure that even your own mother will not recognise your body," said Gabbar.

"Let her go. We don't need to do this," said one of the men who came back to where Gabbar was holding her down.

"You don't need this. I do. This one. She is beautiful," said Gabbar, running his tongue over her forehead.

Jameela felt an immediate urge to puke. Her face contorted with disgust and she began to beg the man again. "Brother, please let me go," she said.

"I told you to STOP calling me brother," he said as he hit her hard between the legs.

Jameela was dazed by the pain from the attack. Gabbar was a foot taller than her and twice as heavy. He drooled all over her face. The look of disgust on her face infuriated him. Gabbar ripped her clothes and ran his hands over her body like a maniac. He quickly lay over her and began to kiss her face.

He was slobbering all over her but she could feel nothing but the pain. The other men came closer. One of them was disgusted but the other man looked like he wanted to join his boss.

"Please," she kept repeating over and over again. At one point, she lost count of how many times and how desperately she had begged him. From that point onwards, Jameela began to hope that this was all a bad dream. She closed her eyes and hoped for it to be over. It seemed like forever. She looked blankly at the cloudless sky without any idea what to do. "Please, brother," she said weakly.

"Damn it," said Gabbar, getting up and zipping his pants. "She just won't stop saying the word," he said and swore loudly. He kicked her in the face and quickly lit a cigarette.

"Should I finish her?" the man who had wanted to join Gabbar asked.

"No," said the other man quickly. Both men turned to him. "Let her go. She won't tell anyone," he said reasonably.

"Let her go? She knows our faces," said the other man.

"Who is she going to tell? Which station would file a case against you? Give her the money and I will ensure she is silent," said the man.

"Money? She ruined my mood by calling me brother

again and again," said Gabbar. He looked furious. He stomped on the ground a couple of times and then ripped Jameela's blouse. "I know your face now. If you even think of telling what happened to anyone, I will murder everyone in your family," he said menacingly.

He walked away but he was furious. He kept shaking his head and cursing. He came towards her furiously and spat on her face. He stubbed his cigarette on her chest. Jameela screamed in pain but he held her throat to silence her.

"Don't kill her, Gabbar," said one of his men, pulling Gabbar away and trying to cool him down. He gestured to his companion to take the woman away before taking Gabbar further away from her.

The other man quickly came over and pulled her away. She could hardly stand up and was dazed by the pain. "Go away quickly before he changes his mind. Forget this happened to you and go," he said as he stuffed her bag into her hands.

There was a long way to go from there along the dark road. It felt even longer as she walked with the pain. She pulled out her shawl from the bag and draped it over herself. Her clothes had been ripped in several places. It was not the cold that hit her. It was something else. She walked aimlessly until she saw someone shining a torch at her. She put her hands in the way of the light to shield her eyes. She could not take any more of this night. She only wanted it to end.

"Jameela! I was worried," came a familiar voice.

"Iqbal!" she said with relief.

"I told you not to use this road. You could have called me. I would have come if you were scared by the dogs. The things you do to scare me. I am glad you will be Nawaz's problem very soon—" he said and stopped abruptly upon seeing her properly. His eyes were wide in horror.

"Take me home, please. I don't want anyone else to see me like this," she whispered weakly.

He looked revolted but he placed his arm over her shoulder and steered her towards their home. His touch scared her momentarily but then gave her the familiar feeling she always had. She was safe now. Iqbal Siddique was a policeman. She did not need to explain what had happened. He knew instantly. She stepped towards the bathroom. She felt unclean.

"Don't lock the door," he said softly. Iqbal was terrified. She did not understand why he said that but she obeyed. She closed the door but did not lock it. She stood under the shower as cold water poured over her. She stood for a long time until Iqbal knocked on the door. She did not feel like responding to him. She still felt unclean. She began to rub herself all over her body. She felt like nothing would be able to clean her.

"Jameela," called Iqbal softly.

She paid him no heed. She could not believe what had just happened to her. She began to panic and breathe heavily. She did not know what drove her to come home. She could not bear the shame of it all.

"Jameela," called Iqbal loudly. He pushed the door slightly and held a towel and a nightie in his hand.

"I am here," she said weakly. She had no idea what to say. She kept soaping herself but she did not seem to be getting clean. The situation just hit her. She had been raped. She looked down at her chest where the animal had stubbed his cigarette. The tears that she had been fighting won the battle. She lay on the floor and bawled her heart out.

Iqbal pushed the door open. Nothing in his entire life had prepared him for this. He wanted to join her and cry his heart out but his instinct drove him to do something else. He turned off the shower, placed the towel around her and pulled her into a warm hug. "It is ok, Jameela," he said weakly, after a very long time.

She leaned over him and began to cry. She cried so hard that she had difficulty breathing. She was not loud but the sound was haunting. Iqbal patted her head and held her close to him. It took some time as she looked pointedly at the door. He gave her fresh clothes and stepped outside.

He kept the door slightly ajar to ensure that she did not do anything to harm herself. It took her a long time but she finally came out. He stood waiting nervously in the living room. She had put on her clothes and she was drying her hair.

He had no idea what to say to her. He had seen many rape victims in his life and he had also consoled a few of them but his mind had gone blank now that the victim was his own flesh and blood. He had no idea what to tell her. He had no idea where to start. Everything that he would do for someone else in the same situation escaped his thoughts.

He had never expected something like this to happen to her. Nothing could have prepared him for this. Jameela waited until she was completely dry. She was determinedly staring away. She did not want to look her brother in the eye.

"We should tell Nawaz," she said abruptly.

"No! Jameela, he must not know about this. The wedding. Everything will be ruined," said Iqbal, clutching his hair. He had only been thinking about her so far. He had forgotten everything else. He had forgotten about the wedding.

"If that happens, so be it. He deserves to know," said Jameela. She placed a hand on his shoulder. "I have cried a lot tonight, Iqbal. I can cry a little more tonight if I have to. He deserves to know," she said calmly.

"Wait till tomorrow. If we call him now, it won't look nice," said Iqbal.

"It isn't late. It is not even eleven. He must be finishing up his shift. I have texted him to come," she said. Iqbal protested but she would not listen. She kept saying that Nawaz deserved to know. Her voice became weaker each time she repeated it.

"Jameela! Take a moment and think about this. You still have not come out of the shock. This was not your fault. If you tell him now, he might call off the whole thing," said Iqbal earnestly. He could not let her life be ruined by this. He would do anything to fix the whole thing.

"I know this isn't my fault. You think that I am not thinking straight but I am. I cannot lie to Nawaz. He deserves to know. I had no choice in what happened to me but Nawaz should have one about this. I cannot start a life with him based on a lie," said Jameela.

"You don't understand. This will ruin your entire life. All that for what? One bad day should not ruin your entire life," said Iqbal. "Please," he added weakly.

"Don't be stupid, Iqbal. The entire time I cried, I was only thinking about what I could have done differently," she began nervously.

"Don't go there. Don't blame yourself. That will only make things worse," said Iqbal immediately. As he was speaking, he heard the sound of a scooter approaching their house. He moved between Jameela and the door. He wanted to stop this but Nawaz was already at the door. "I can tell him to go. I can tell him that you fell asleep. I can lie," he began as he pleaded with her.

"You did not lie to him when they approached us. Don't start now, Iqbal," said Jameela firmly. She tried to sound firm but she was nervous. She liked Nawaz too much to hide this from him. Though she wanted to be honest with him, she did not know if she could handle him walking out on her. She stared at the floor nervously.

Iqbal wanted to protect her from all this but it was too late. Nawaz was already at the gate. He looked at her sadly as she stood there, looking at Nawaz. She was not fighting tears anymore. She was looking at the floor with a blank expression on her face.

Nawaz had a chocolate bar in his hand and grinned as he saw Iqbal. He quickly removed his shoes and went to the bathroom to wash his feet. "Don't tell my parents that I came here," he said sheepishly as he stepped outside the bathroom a few minutes later. He was a handsome man and he was blushing.

His moustache and beard were neatly trimmed as always. He took a good look at his bride-to-be and her brother. Something seemed wrong. They looked like they were in shock. Jameela's message had been very short. "What happened? Is something wrong?" Nawaz asked slowly.

Jameela had been confident that she had to tell Nawaz about her ordeal. Now that he was here, she could not get herself to say a word. She couldn't get a single word out of her mouth. She looked at her brother, who was looking at her anxiously.

"I thought you wanted to meet me but you look

like you've been—" he said, walking close to Jameela. She shuddered and took a step back, almost like it was a reflex. Iqbal, who had been putting on a brave face till then, closed his eyes and turned around. Nawaz looked at Jameela. She stood in a nighty and her hair was still wet.

Nawaz worked in the casualty ward in the hospital. He had seen every type of injury in the book. He also knew how people reacted after trauma. He had seen enough people to know what had happened to her. He could not believe it but it had happened to Jameela. He stood open-mouthed in horror.

Jameela and Iqbal were looking at each other and fighting the urge to cry. He had seen this far too many times. He walked close to Jameela and pulled her into a hug. "It's okay. It is not your fault," he said, making a whole-hearted effort to not break down. She struggled to get out of the hug but he held her firmly until she relaxed in his arms. "Shut every door and window," he hissed at Iqbal. Iqbal obeyed meekly.

He had seen Jameela cry once already that day. It had been the worst thing he had ever seen in his life. That did not prepare him for what came next. It was louder and more painful to watch. Nawaz made her sit without breaking the hug. She leaned over him and began to weep.

She tried to speak but she could not put two words together. She continued to cry for a long time. This time, she was quieter and coherent. She fell asleep, leaning on Nawaz, tired from the crying.

"Are you ok?" Nawaz asked. He placed a hand on Iqbal's knees. Iqbal stood a few feet away from his sister, not taking his eyes off her.

"I have seen a few cases but I never thought I would—" said Iqbal, clenching his fists with anger. He was beginning to see red.

"I know. I guess nothing really prepares you for something like this. Are you ok to help me?" Nawaz asked politely.

"Help with what?" Iqbal asked, looking at him with surprise.

"She has been raped," said Nawaz. He paused for a moment to compose himself. This was the first time since she had reached home that the word was used. He took a few minutes to regain his voice. "I need you to get a few items. You can get these in any pharmacy. Go to a pharmacy where they don't know you," said Nawaz.

"What? Why?" Iqbal asked.

"She needs medical attention. I have to give it to her. I want it to be discreet," said Nawaz as he typed the names of medicines and other items into his phone. "I have texted you the details. Get back as soon as you can," said Nawaz.

"Okay," said Iqbal. He had not thought of getting her help. They had been too shocked to even think about something like this.

"Will you be okay going out on your own?" Nawaz asked.

"I will be fine. I am a policeman," said Iqbal, gaining composure. He quickly took his keys and his wallet and left to get the items. He got the items from three different pharmacies, in parts, just to ensure that nobody would doubt him. He realised that Nawaz had not panicked as much as him.

He realised that a man who was not yet his family was acting more mature than him in this situation. His respect for the man grew. He then realised that Nawaz could still choose to end everything when he got home. His sister's life was ruined due to no fault of her own. He could not take these thoughts off his mind. He realised that she was going through something much worse than him. He could not even imagine her pain. He drove home faster and gave the package to Nawaz.

"Keep that away for now. We need to first get her comfortable," said Nawaz.

"Did she say something?" Iqbal asked slowly.

"She hasn't gotten up since you left," said Nawaz.

Iqbal knew what they had to do. Nawaz wanted to treat her medically but she had to be prepared for that mentally. He had no words to say to Nawaz. He was surprised just by the presence of the man. It did not take long for Jameela to wake up. By the time she was awake, Iqbal was mentally prepared for what would come next.

Both men had experience dealing with victims of such crimes. Yet, both men proceeded nervously. They had never been involved with the victim emotionally and that changed everything.

It took them almost an hour to get the details out of her. Jameela gave them the gist of what had happened and the details of her attacker. She knew Gabbar but she did not know the two men with him. After talking for a little more time, Jameela allowed Nawaz to treat her. Nawaz told him that he was going to give her a sedative to take a long rest and that he did not see any lasting damage from the ordeal. He mentioned that he would get her treated discreetly. Iqbal stood outside as he treated her, pacing around angrily.

Gabbar had done this to his sister. He was a filthy animal. He had been tormenting people for far too long. This had to end. He wanted to avenge his sister. He did not need much time to decide what he wanted to do. He walked back into his house. As he entered, he saw Jameela lying down with her eyes closed.

Nawaz gently placed his hand on her forehead, looking at her fondly. Iqbal knew that he was doing the right thing. This man would be there for his sister. He convinced himself that he was doing the right thing. He went to his room and opened the safe within his cupboard. He kept his service revolver there.

He took it and stuffed it into his pocket. As he stepped out of the room, Nawaz was already in the hall.

He had been calmer than Iqbal so far but he was finally showing emotion. Iqbal wanted to console him but he did not want to waste time.

"Where are you going?" Nawaz asked as he saw Iqbal reach the door.

"Outside," said Iqbal.

"Where?" Nawaz asked sharply.

"Just outside," said Iqbal.

"Don't be a fool, Iqbal," said Nawaz calmly.

"What?" Iqbal asked with surprise.

"I saw you take the gun," said Nawaz calmly.

"She is my sister," hissed Iqbal angrily.

"She is my wife. Married or not, I see Jameela as my wife," said Nawaz.

"I cannot let him live," said Iqbal through gritted teeth.

"What do you think this will accomplish?" Nawaz asked.

"What do you mean? I must kill that animal. He hurt my sister," said Iqbal.

"How can you be so selfish?" Nawaz asked angrily.

"Me? Selfish?" Iqbal asked; he could not digest this remark.

"Go! Go and kill him. What will you do after that?" Nawaz asked. Iqbal stood silently. He had no answer. "Did you think what this will do to your sister?" Nawaz asked calmly, after taking a long look at Iqbal.

"I can't let him go. I cannot arrest him also. The

legal proceedings will take forever and Jameela will have to relive this so many times. I cannot let that happen to her. The judgment of those around us—I cannot even imagine how bad that will be. They will blame her for what that animal did to her. Her clothes and job will be reason enough for the people. The only way is to shoot Gabbar like the dog that he is," said Iqbal.

"Why do you care about the opinion of others? What about how this will affect your sister? Everyone will find out why you killed him. Even if we somehow manage to hide your reasons, she will have to watch you go to jail. She will have to go through that without you," said Nawaz and opened the door.

"He is the animal and you want to destroy our lives for that? Go! Think about how you are going to literally end your life and your career for a lowlife. Once you understand that fully, go and shoot him," said Nawaz.

"I can't let him live. Not after what he did. He does not deserve to live," said Iqbal.

"I agree. He does not deserve to live. Do you deserve to lose your life? Does your sister deserve to lose you?" Nawaz asked.

"He must die," said Iqbal.

"I don't deny that. I just don't agree with your method," said Nawaz.

"What do you mean?" Iqbal asked.

"You are a policeman. Think like one," said Nawaz.

"That is why I am ending him. The proceedings

will destroy her more than the incident," said Iqbal.

Nawaz took a deep breath. Iqbal was not able to understand. "You need to kill him but you should not be implicated. You can have your vengeance but not at the cost of our lives. I say 'our' because what you do will affect everyone," said Nawaz.

Iqbal went in to make sure that Jameela was asleep. She was sound asleep and he adjusted her blankets. Iqbal wished he could turn the clock back. This should never have happened. With a heavy heart, he walked back to the hall.

"Nobody needs to know about this," said Nawaz.

"We will be discreet obviously but your parents?" Iqbal asked.

"They are good people but they won't understand this. You were right when you spoke about people judging her. We still live in a society where the woman will be blamed for being raped. I will not let Jameela go through that," said Nawaz.

"You are ok with this?" Iqbal asked slowly.

"I wouldn't think any less of my wife if she got bitten by a dog. This is no different. I love her. She loves me. That is the only thing that matters," said Nawaz, tearing up.

Iqbal pulled Nawaz into a tight hug. He could not imagine what the young man was going through but he was surer now than ever that he could not have found a better groom for his sister.

"This doesn't end with this. We are going to have to get her help," said Nawaz as they sat at the doorstep an hour later. Nawaz sighed and sipped his coffee.

"What do you mean?" Iqbal asked.

"The physical aspects of it and the medication, I can take care of that. She is going to need to get psychiatric help," said Nawaz.

"What? Why?" Iqbal asked.

"This is going to hurt her mentally more than physically. These kinds of things cause emotional trauma and we need to be there for her," said Nawaz.

"I'll do anything necessary," said Iqbal.

"It is not just that. You need to find a psychiatrist who can be discreet. There are doctors who will want you to file a complaint before they begin treating her. We need to find someone we trust to handle this. She is going to need help. Before that, we need to convince her that she needs help," said Nawaz.

"I don't know how to do any of that," said Iqbal, looking at the floor. Every moment, he was feeling worse than the last. His sister was going to have to go through so much due to no fault of her own. "Why her? She never harmed anyone," said Iqbal angrily.

"Most people never do. This is just bad luck. Sometimes, bad things happen to good people," said Nawaz.

"I want you to tell me what I need to look for and when. I will do whatever you say," said Iqbal, convincing himself. As he calmed down, he saw the pain in Nawaz's face.

"I have a few doctors in mind. I will ask around. We need to get her help as soon as possible. I will pick someone and get the earliest appointment. I want you to hold everything until we get her the help," said Nawaz, looking at Iqbal seriously.

"Sure," said Iqbal.

"I want you to promise me that you won't do anything stupid," said Nawaz.

Iqbal stared at him for a long time and then slowly nodded. Iqbal wanted to do nothing more than hunt Gabbar down immediately but he saw that Nawaz was right. He nodded again to reassure him.

"This is more important than revenge or anything else that will make you feel better. This is not about you or me. We need to get her the help she needs immediately. The sooner, the better. I have read a lot of studies on this. This is complicated," said Nawaz.

Iqbal nodded. He was going to do whatever Nawaz said. When he finished all that, he would go after Gabbar. He would make the animal pay for what he had done to Jameela. In less than a day, their whole world had been shattered.

CHAPTER 14

HUNTING A PREDATOR

Iqbal had spent a lot of time researching Gabbar and his gang. The two men who were always with him were Hemant and Blade. He had to check very discreetly but he found that they were the same two men who were with Gabbar when he had attacked Jameela. Being from the same area, it was easy for him to track them. Iqbal knew that this fact would help him evade any suspicion. Nawaz had a good point. He wanted vengeance but not at the cost of their lives.

In a few days, he came to know Gabbar's schedule by heart but he found that Gabbar was almost never alone. He had men with him at all times. Blade, in particular, was like his shadow. He was with Gabbar even when Gabbar was with his mistress. Iqbal was repulsed by this fact. Gabbar's mistress was Blade's sister.

Iqbal was patiently watching Gabbar every day. That was when he heard from Nawaz that Blade was supposed to travel to his native place to sell some property. It was easy to isolate him and finish him off.

Jameela told him that one of Gabbar's companions was not as bad as the other.

He did not know which one amongst Blade and Hemant was the good one. It did not matter. He could not afford to let this come back to him. Both men assisted a rapist without remorse. They deserved death.

He asked Blade to meet him by the marina. He met him casually and mentioned to him that he wanted a property and that he was interested in what he was selling. Blade came expecting to get a deal done but Iqbal had other ideas. He had chosen a place where nobody could see them.

He kept speaking to him normally to lead him to a secluded spot. A quick cut to the neck was enough to subdue him. He could not raise his voice to call for help. Iqbal beat him with a rock a few times to vent out his anger. Once he was done with him, he tied him to a heavy rock he had found nearby with a rope that he had carried with him.

He tied the body, which was held underwater by the rock, to a fishing boat, hoping that he would be taken deep into the sea. He expected the body to be lost at sea but his plan backfired with the body turning up in the marina. But by the time it turned up, he had finished Gabbar. He ensured that he was the first person on the scene when Blade's body turned up. It gave him a great deal of satisfaction to kill Blade with his own hand.

Once he had killed Blade, he knew that he would

not have much time to finish Gabbar. Sooner or later, they would realise that he was missing. Iqbal also needed a strong alibi in case something went wrong. He faked an accident involving him and his sister. He advised her to stay at home and got Nawaz to bandage him believably.

Nawaz was fully with him in this effort but they made the choice to keep Jameela out of this. She did not have to know what they were doing. She had suffered enough. Applying for medical leave, Iqbal began to make arrangements for the next phase of his plan. He roamed around with his bandages just to make sure that people knew about his injury.

He had planned to isolate Gabbar at the edge of the marina well in advance. He took every precaution he could think of. He knew how the department worked. He planned everything meticulously. He could not afford any witnesses to the murder. He had to isolate Gabbar, which was next to impossible.

He kept monitoring Gabbar patiently when he noticed his regular route. He knew that Gabbar was going drinking that night. He wanted to force them to take the route where they would be stopped by patrol officers. He moved a barricade in their usual route to block them and placed some stones to ensure that it would be difficult to move it.

Every person who was with Gabbar was drunk. Iqbal was watching as they tried to move the barricade.

He had hoped that they would not succeed. They did not. They were too drunk to take the effort. Iqbal knew that he would be called when they were caught at the check-post. Right on schedule, he got the call.

The officers at the check-post were unsure what to do. None of them wanted to arrest Gabbar but they were not ready to let them drive this way. There was a lot of bad press due to police not being strict with drunk drivers in the recent past. Like any normal policeman would, he advised them to hold the vehicle and Gabbar's companions but he told them to let Gabbar go.

Iqbal knew that he had to scare anyone from coming to the spot where he had planned the kill. He had a clever plan. He draped a white saree around him and wore a wig and began to walk along the deserted road. He noticed one or two people at a distance seeing him and running away. There was a rumour in the area about Bhadra. There were multiple interpretations about Bhadra but the most common one was that of a woman in a white saree and long hair roaming in the nights.

He knew that Gabbar's gang exploited this rumour. Gabbar had his men run around in this disguise when he had shady activities in progress in the area. Iqbal knew that this was the best way to get Gabbar. Everyone in the marina had reason to fear Bhadra except Gabbar. Iqbal expected this to help him avoid unnecessary crowd and put Gabbar at ease. There were several other alleged sightings of the ghost but Iqbal did not believe in any of them.

It took a long time for Gabbar to come there. Iqbal was waiting for him. Gabbar was extremely drunk. That would make Iqbal's job much easier. He watched as Gabbar turned and walked in the opposite direction. He wanted to attract his attention. As luck would have it, Gabbar turned and noticed him.

Once he did, everything fell into place. He waited until Gabbar came close to him. He struck him hard on his temple. He then hit him hard on his throat and jammed his voice box. Gabbar fought back but he could not do much damage in his intoxicated state.

Iqbal would never forget anything that happened after that. That memory would stay with him for the rest of his life. He grabbed a sharp stone and struck Gabbar all over his body until his arms were tired. Gabbar could not scream but he could feel the pain despite being drunk. Iqbal struck him for a long time.

When he stopped, Gabbar was long dead and his arm was hurting him. He looked around for any clues that he could have left. There was not much he could do in the darkness. He quickly took off his disguise and took a much longer route home after disposing off his disguise in different parts of the city to avoid anything getting traced back to him.

When he reached home, his right forearm had swollen. It began to hurt a lot. Nawaz got him treated.

The X-ray revealed a hairline fracture. The report was pre-dated to coincide with his accident and he got a real sling for his arm.

He would never forget the expression on Jameela's face when she heard the news about Gabbar's death. She was watching the coverage with interest. She felt both happy and relieved that her tormentor was dead. Iqbal could do nothing to take that painful memory away but this was the next best thing. Jameela was watching every news channel one after the other. There was a satisfied expression on her face. Iqbal felt like everything he had done was worth the risk.

Gabbar's death gave him a great deal of satisfaction. It was vengeance but he felt like he had accomplished something big. He knew that he had to kill the other person who was with Gabbar on that night but that would be difficult now. Gabbar's death had made everyone alert. Hemant was his final target and he was spooked.

Iqbal knew that the best part of the murder was that nobody knew that it was him. Nobody had any reason to suspect him. If he finished Hemant, he could take the secret of that night to his grave. He wanted to stay close to the investigation of the case but he was not sure who would take the lead on such a high-profile case.

He debated whether to join the investigation or to stay away from it. After much thought, he decided that it was better to be a part of the investigation even if someone else was running it. That way, he could steer it away from him in the off chance that he had made any mistakes so far.

With his arm being fractured, he had to postpone the third murder. To add to it, Hemant had disappeared. He was somewhere within the area but Iqbal had not been able to find him. As he sat thinking about killing Gabbar, he received the phone call. It was not unexpected but he could not help but laugh as he realised that he would be a part of the investigation where he was the killer they were searching for. As he reached the scene, he realised that he did not know anything about Gaurav Singh, the officer leading the investigation.

Given the sensitive nature of the murder, they had brought in a specialist. Iqbal felt that this was best. He did not have any liability but he could subtly lead the investigation away from him should the need arise. Over the course of the investigation, he felt relieved knowing that Gaurav Singh was brought in to minimise violence rather than find the killer.

He enquired around and got to know that Gaurav was very good at what he did but he was with them to negotiate a truce. Iqbal felt that this was god's way of helping him for doing a good deed. Gabbar deserved to die for all the people he had hurt.

The investigation was proceeding briskly but it was leading away from him. Iqbal remained calm and behaved like his usual self. He helped Gaurav in whatever way he had to while keeping himself apprised of the situation. Gaurav was thinking like a policeman. He was looking at usual suspects. He was quite efficient and was able to get information from different sources. Iqbal did nothing that could divert him.

Gaurav was trying to broker peace and he was being forced to do it speedily by his superiors. This favoured Iqbal's cause. While he had got his vengeance, the murder could lead to a lot of violence on the streets. Iqbal worked tirelessly to ensure that civilians were not affected. He knew that the murder was right but he had to bear the consequences of it.

The first risk came when they went after Hemant. He tried to be a part of the team that would chase him but Gaurav refused to include him due to his injury. Iqbal began to panic. The entire case was now closing around him. Everyone was under the impression that Hemant was the killer. If they caught Hemant, there was a good chance that Gaurav would realise that he was innocent.

Even if Hemant could not link this to Iqbal, he could talk about the rape during his interrogation. Iqbal kept pacing around anxiously when he noticed the writer at their station. He had known for years that this man was paid by Rajan and he was extremely loyal to Baaji. He decided to do the only thing that he could. He made it look like he accidentally spilled the information about Hemant in the writer's vicinity.

The writer was so loyal that he wasted almost no time in informing Baaji. He knew how Baaji would think. He would either want to catch him before the police could or he would want him dead. Either way, Hemant would not survive this chase. The police were already in the area and the only way this would end was his death.

Iqbal sat listening to the police scanners and realised that the police were close to losing him. Wasting no time, he made a call from a phone in the station to Hemant and warned him that they were closing in on him. He had anticipated that Hemant would prefer death over getting caught by either party and he was right.

He heard the news of Hemant's death from Gaurav who called to inform him about the unexpected change of events. Iqbal quietly removed Hemant's phone from the evidence and destroyed it. With that phone gone, there was no evidence linking him to the case. With all three members gone, his vengeance was complete. He could go back to his life.

This case would be closed soon. Gaurav was a senior policeman. He would not want to be bothered with the paperwork. Iqbal could alter the paperwork to suit his agenda and close this case. He could get away with two kills and an important role in a third and get some credit for it within the department.

Iqbal spent the next few days keeping his eyes and ears open for any loose ends. There were none but he wanted to stay alert just in case. That was when he heard the writer call Baaji. One of their informants from the streets had told them that Isaac from Cyrus' gang was claiming to have ordered the hit on Gabbar.

Iqbal knew right away that this man had a death wish. This was a stupid move that would get him killed. The information had reached Baaji before he could do anything. He kept pacing around nervously, realising that more people were going to be killed. He had no qualms about the three people who were dead.

They were animals and they deserved what they got but he felt uncomfortable about violence spilling over to the streets. He felt responsible. After thinking for a while, a realisation hit him. None of these men were innocent. Every single person leading each of these gangs was a hardened criminal.

The city would only become safe with them out of the picture. He realised that there was a way to take them both out of the equation. He had a few friends in the traffic control department. He knew that they had cameras all over the city. He made an excuse to visit an old friend who worked in the control room.

A lot of people visited the office and there was no entry register unlike several other important departments. There was very little security around traffic monitoring.

He spotted the feed for the camera that was close to the market area where he knew Baaji would try to attack Cyrus and his gang. His friend in the control room had very little awareness about cyber safety. His username and password to the system was written on a small piece of paper, which he kept under his keyboard.

Iqbal kept checking the cameras. The murder happened in the evening and that was when the people in the control room realised that one of their cameras was pointed in the wrong direction. Several people including Iqbal witnessed the murder live. Iqbal realised that the department could attempt to suppress this information too.

He did not want a cold-blooded murderer like Baaji walking free. If nothing else, keeping him off the streets would make the marina a better place. He snuck into the control room later that evening and made a few copies of the video. He quickly packed them in packages while ensuring that there were no prints on any of them.

He personally delivered them to a few media houses in the city, hoping that at least one of them would run the news. If one of them did, all of them would follow suit. It did not take long for them to go live with the video. This was too good for them to miss. Iqbal felt glad that a gangster was killed and another gangster would be arrested with irrefutable evidence. Not even Rajan could help Baaji escape this mess with such damning evidence.

Everything after that had gone smoothly. The

paperwork pointed to Hemant. With Hemant dead, the reports said that Cyrus and his gang were probably behind the hit. This had prompted Baaji to retaliate. Now, Baaji was injured and he would spend a long time in jail. Iqbal felt content knowing that he had his revenge and the city was better for it.

Iqbal did not regret anything. If he had to do everything all over again, he wouldn't think twice. His conscience was clear and the animals who had hurt his sister were dead. He had achieved his vengeance without risking his life and career.

CHAPTER 15

A CONFRONTATION

4:30 PM (PRESENT DAY)

Gaurav was going over the paperwork. He had a hunch and as unbelievable as it was, everything was fitting in. The register had Iqbal Siddique's signature from when he had applied for leave. The thing that caught Gaurav's attention was the comments column. No policeman ever filled that column.

This was a register which was completely useless and it was unofficial. The only person to make an entry in that column in a long time was Iqbal Siddique. It was mentioned that he had fractured his left arm. Gaurav vividly remembered Siddique wearing a sling on his right arm. He had a hunch that this was someone from the department and he could not let it go. He had spent more than five hours cracking the case.

The entry would not have mattered much but when Gaurav checked with his superiors, he found out that Siddique had texted them that his left arm was injured. Even if the entry register was an honest mistake, it was not usual for anyone to make the same mistake twice. Siddique had never entered comments during any of his previous leaves.

It looked that the detail was unnecessary and out of place. Gaurav knew immediately that he had to follow this lead discreetly. He did not want to spook Siddique. Siddique had been smart. He had covered his bases well and made it look like a gang murder. The first part that gave him away was the writer. Gaurav cornered him and casually asked him how he had passed the information about Hemant to Baaji. The writer did not even seem taken aback.

"That guy with the broken arm was blabbing," he said happily.

It was unlike Siddique but Gaurav remained quiet. He did not want the writer to leak any more of the department's secrets. He faked a laugh and walked away. Siddique had lied about his injury but his right arm was now legitimately injured. He had been involved in something around the time Gabbar was killed. Nobody was ready to check the DNA evidence around Gabbar's body but Gaurav was sure that some of that would lead to Siddique.

The next thing that reaffirmed his doubts were the phone records of Hemant's phone. His phone was lost but his phone records were not. The last call he had taken when he was alive was from the police station and it was from the empty cabin next to the conference room. There was no way to prove that Siddique was the one who had made the call but Siddique was in the office and nobody could dispute that.

Gaurav checked with the traffic control room. Siddique had a few friends in the office and he had been around the control room several times during that period. Multiple people could place him there. While the news about the leak had been suppressed to avoid any problems, Gaurav found out that the data was copied after normal working hours. There was no way to confirm who did it but he did not have many suspects.

Siddique was a policeman and he had the skills to track Gabbar and take him on. He could be placed near two important sites—the office from where Hemant was called, and the traffic room from where a murder footage was leaked. None of these were solid evidence against Iqbal but it fit Gaurav's suspicions.

Gaurav began to go over the events and realised that Siddique could have realistically done this. Siddique was from the area and he had lived there all his life. Nobody would have suspected a policeman in this kind of a case but Siddique had good knowledge of the area. That put a lot of things in perspective.

Gaurav did not want to believe it but if Siddique really had killed Gabbar, he had been incredibly lucky to be a part of the investigation. Not only was he a part of the investigation but he had also done the paperwork.

That gave him ample of chances to doctor the evidence and erase traces of his involvement.

One thing struck out. Siddique had no motive to murder Gabbar or influence any of the events that followed the murder. Siddique was no vigilante and he was someone who preferred to keep a low profile. He did not take any risks on the job and this seemed totally out of character. All hunches pointed to Siddique but there was no evidence that showed a clear motive for the murder.

"Where is Siddique?" Gaurav asked one of the constables. He wanted to confront Siddique but he was not sure how he was going to question him. He had no proper proof and he had reached a conclusion based on a series of hunches.

"The sub-inspector said that he would be back soon. He had some personal work," said the constable, not even bothering to stifle his yawn. "He said he wanted to go to some hospital," he added lazily.

"Is he sick?" Gaurav asked doubtfully.

"I'm not sure. He must be," said the constable indifferently.

***

4:50 PM

Gaurav decided to question him another day when he had a clear idea of what could have happened.

Confronting Siddique without any evidence was not going to end well. Everything that had caused him to suspect Siddique was circumstantial. As he drove towards the governor's office, he saw Siddique walking with a woman.

He was holding her hand and speaking to her calmly. The woman looked sullen but she kept nodding at him. He then put his hands on her shoulder and smiled at her. After a bit of reluctance, she returned the smile. Gaurav saw that he was coming out of the government hospital complex.

Gaurav asked his driver to go into the hospital complex. He knew that it was better to get the full story before talking to Siddique. What he had was no trivial suspicion. He was suspecting a fellow policeman of multiple murders. That was a scandal in itself. Considering the magnitude of the case that they had closed, it was unimaginable.

Gaurav walked into the hospital and began to enquire about Siddique's presence. He was being directed towards the east wing of the hospital when he overheard a conversation.

"She is a tough woman, Nawaz," said a female voice.

"She is, Doctor. Is she going to be fine?" Nawaz asked, sounding concerned. Gaurav noticed that a doctor was talking with a male nurse.

"You got her here at the right time. Physically, she is

fine already. Two or three more sessions and she should be much better mentally. Once we do that, she can stop the regular sessions with me. You are a good man, Nawaz. Most people think that seeking mental help is a weakness," said the doctor appreciatively. Gaurav took a quick look at her before going back to staying out of view.

"That is all I wanted to hear, Doctor. I don't know how to thank you. Not many would have agreed to keep it off the books," said Nawaz, sounding thankful.

"Nonsense! This is the least I could do for another woman. Just to imagine what she had gone through. I am only surprised that she did not get a look at her attackers," said the doctor, shaking her head.

"It was dark and we tried our best to get her to remember," said Nawaz.

"With her brother being a policeman, all you needed was some clue and these animals would be behind bars," said the woman with a sigh. "Maybe it is for the best. This way, she can move on. As her fiancée, you have exceeded expectations," said the doctor kindly.

Gaurav remained quiet. He was still making the connection but he had figured out most of the things. The woman who was with Siddique was his sister. This man, Nawaz, was her fiancée. He quickly gathered information on the doctor. She was Stella Johnson, a psychiatrist who specialised in trauma counselling.

Based on the conversation, Siddique's sister

was attacked by a group of people. Siddique was a policeman. He had the means to go after someone who attacked his own family. If the attackers were Gabbar and his goons, Siddique had motive.

"Oh god!" Gaurav said, as he pieced everything together.

***

8:30 PM (THE NEXT DAY)

Gaurav waited in the route frequented by Iqbal Siddique on his way home. He was going over everything he had found in the last two days. He knew everything there was to know now. He was unsure how he felt about this. Iqbal Siddique had taken the law into his own hands and his actions had resulted in so many deaths.

What happened to Iqbal's family was unimaginable but his vengeance was unbelievable. He had asked his driver to leave him and stood leaning on his car by the side of the road.

Siddique was a few minutes late but he noticed Gaurav and stopped his vehicle. His sling was gone but he still had a crepe bandage on his hand. He parked his vehicle and gave Gaurav a customary salute.

"I am sorry I could not see you at the office. Was the paperwork to your satisfaction?" he asked sincerely.

"It was very detailed but that is not why I am here," said Gaurav slowly. He did not want to spook Siddique yet.

"I don't understand," said Siddique, feigning surprise.

"You remember my doubts on someone from the department behind Gabbar's murder?" Gaurav asked, trying to remain casual.

"Yes. The DCP was not pleased with that," said Siddique pointedly. Gaurav noticed that Siddique was nervous but he was trying his best to remain calm. "Are you still pursuing that angle, Sir?"

"I am not," said Gaurav. Siddique relaxed a bit on hearing it. "I know now for sure that it was done by one of our own," added Gaurav immediately. Siddique looked at Gaurav with bewilderment, unsure of how to react.

"Someone from our department did all this?" he asked, sounding serious but Gaurav was looking at the sub-inspector. There was no need to doubt his hunch now. Siddique was guilty and he was cornered.

"You tell me," said Gaurav.

It dawned on Siddique that he was now cornered. He remained silent but he kept looking around. There was a silver lining. Gaurav was alone and there was no other policeman in sight. He was thinking of something to say but he knew that speaking would only make things worse. He did not regret what he did but it was not over until it was over. He wanted Gaurav to say the actual words to believe it.

"Do you want to know where you messed up?" Gaurav asked sharply. He had been a policeman for long enough to understand Siddique's expression. He knew that Siddique knew that he was cornered.

"Does it matter?" Siddique asked indifferently.

"What do you mean?" Gaurav asked, taken aback by the response.

"You cannot prove anything. The case is closed and it will stay that way," said Siddique softly but it looked like he was unsure about what he was saying.

"You can't expect to live with this," said Gaurav earnestly.

"You will be surprised what people can live with," said Siddique scathingly. He was now confident that Gaurav had nothing on him.

"Your actions led to the death of so many people. Think of the families of those people. Parents have lost sons, wives have lost husbands and—" began Gaurav.

"Think of how many sons and husbands these people have killed. Think of the crimes they are responsible for. I am not saying that I killed them. I am saying this in case you are recording me. I did not kill them but I don't regret what happened. The city is better without these animals," said Siddique sharply. He looked at Gaurav cautiously.

Gaurav realised that Siddique was covering his bases. Recording him illegally would not count as evidence in court but Siddique knew the risk of being caught on tape. "I'll report you," said Gaurav seriously.

"Who will believe you? The case is closed and all

the evidence has been checked. Nothing points to me," asked Siddique.

"You forget that I am a policeman. As smart as you are, I will find a way to trap you," said Gaurav sharply.

"Give it your best shot. You will only make a fool of yourself," said Siddique confidently. He had doctored the evidence to let him walk out of this.

"You are a policeman and you killed a man in cold blood. Admit it!" Gaurav said.

"I won't admit to anything. If you really think I killed him, prove it! Besides, it is not like the person who died is Mahatma Gandhi. Gabbar was a second generation lowlife who harmed the city more than he should have been allowed to," said Siddique dismissively.

"That is beside the point. You are a policeman. You took an oath to protect and serve," said Gaurav, trying to appeal to the young man.

"We are supposed to protect and serve. Answer me honestly. Who are we really protecting or serving?" Siddique said.

"That is not our decision," said Gaurav angrily. "This department is run by people who know better than you. They know the consequences and they obey the law. These are people—"

"Who runs them? Who runs the people who make decisions for us?" Siddique asked, looking at Gaurav seriously. "You still believe in a system that is broken beyond hope. They can kill, extort and do much more with no hindrance. The worst part is that we will salute them as they become the leaders of this country. I have no love lost for Gabbar. The world is better with him dead. If you think I killed him, prove it. I dare you! I have nothing else to say to you but know this—I will not go down in silence," he said in a tone of warning.

"I know what Gabbar did," said Gaurav.

The colour drained from Siddique's face. He wanted to act like he was confused but his face had said all that Gaurav wanted to see.

"You don't know anything. You are talking rubbish," said Siddique immediately but his fists were clenched.

"Am I?" Gaurav asked.

"I am sure you are. Why else would you accuse me of being involved in the murder of the most powerful man in my area?" Siddique asked calmly.

"I know what happened to your sister," repeated Gaurav.

Siddique did not reply. He had no idea what to say. He racked his brain but he had no idea how to respond. If Gaurav knew this, it was game over. If the information ever got out, their lives were over. Jameela would have to live through the experience over and over again for the rest of her life. This was in addition to whatever Rajan would do to them.

Gaurav was not corrupt. If he knew this, he was not going to let it go for money or anything material. He could attack Gaurav but he did not want to. Gaurav was an honest man. Gaurav was only doing his job. He had a justifiable cause to finish Gabbar and his mates but if he started taking innocent lives, he would be no different than those he had killed.

"Leave her out of this," said Siddique desperately.

"Jameela doesn't know, does she?" Gaurav asked knowingly. Siddique did not answer but Gaurav knew it just by seeing the man's face. "What about her fiancée?" Gaurav asked as he took his phone and began checking his messages.

"He has nothing to do with this," said Siddique. He still stood by what he did. He believed that he had doctored the evidence sufficiently to ensure that it could never point to him. Despite doing all that right, he was unsure how Gaurav was confronting him about the murder that he had strived so hard to hide his involvement in. He tried to think of a mistake that he could have made but nothing struck his mind.

"You can go home, Siddique," said Gaurav.

"What?" Siddique asked in disbelief. He was not sure if he had heard him right. "Are you not going to arrest me?" he asked slowly.

"Not this time, no. It is not just because of the chaos this could create. I don't agree with what you did but I understand why. It isn't right. Nobody should take the law into their own hands but I think you have suffered enough. I will sign the paperwork and forget this case," said Gaurav gravely.

"Are you sure?" Siddique asked. He did not realise what he said until after he had said it. It felt so stupid. Gaurav was letting him walk away from the murder.

"This case is closed for the greater good. I can open it and create more chaos but I don't want to do that. I am going back to my job at the governor's office and you can go back to your life. Go now. Go before I change my mind," said Gaurav.

He did not want to say anything else. Gaurav was not sure why he was saying this but he felt like he was doing the right thing. This was not about Siddique doing the right thing. This was about peace in the city. That was his job. He was a master in negotiating truce and this was the only way to ensure that peace in the city would last.

"I will be watching you. If you ever try any funny business, I will put you behind bars irrespective of the consequences," said Gaurav, hoping that he had done enough to stop Siddique from indulging in more vigilantism.

Siddique looked at Gaurav with a shocked expression. He saw that Gaurav meant what he said. He had been very careful in executing his plan but Gaurav had caught on. If he did, then someone else could. With his seniority and influence in the department, Gaurav would have no trouble proving his suspicion. Had it been someone else, Siddique would not have thought twice about killing him too. Gaurav was a good man.

He was only doing his job.

Siddique wanted to say 'Thank you' but it did not feel right. He looked at Gaurav, who signalled him to leave quickly.

Gaurav watched as Siddique drove away. He kept looking back at Gaurav as he moved away but did not make eye-contact. It was obvious that he was nervous. Gaurav kept looking at him with a serious look on his face. He had seen plenty of crimes but he could not imagine what Siddique would have gone through that night.

What he had done was wrong. It was against the law but Gaurav did not know if he would have acted differently if he had been in the same situation. Siddique had planned and executed this very well. The solution to the case was a forced fit but it was one that was for the greater good.

Any action Gaurav took on him would harm Siddique and his family. It would also disturb the peace which had been obtained out of sheer luck. That would trigger a war between Rajan and the police. It would be worse than the war he had been called in to help avoid.

Gaurav took a deep breath and walked back to his car. He put the case out of his mind and decided to go back to his family. He only wished that the city became safer for people like Siddique's sister. If the police could not protect their own family, he wondered what good they were doing.

He did not know if Siddique would go back to being

an honest cop but he decided to trust him. Siddique had walked free from his crime but Gaurav wanted Siddique to believe that he would be watching him. Crimes were as different as the criminals themselves. Gaurav knew this better than anyone else, having been in the department for so long. Whatever Siddique did after this was on him. Gaurav only hoped that he would never come to regret his decision.

***

4:55 PM (THE PREVIOUS DAY)

Angel sat staring at Nawaz who was walking with a woman. The woman looked tired as she boarded the auto-rickshaw. Nawaz looked very serious. Yet, there was tenderness in the way he helped her. Behind Nawaz, there was a policeman with a bandage on his hands. He had a concerned look on his face. The moment she saw them together, a thought struck her mind.

Nawaz knew exactly how she felt about Blade and Gabbar. That did not worry her. What worried her was the timeline when they met and the events that followed. Nawaz had asked her about her brother's land and her brother was going to meet a local buyer who was a policeman.

It was not too hard to figure out the details after that. This was the same policeman who had come to Rajan's house. He was part of the investigation. The details could win her Rajan's favour eternally. She did not even want to think about it.

If she was right, things would be so different for them. She did not know why but she decided to forget them. Her brother's death did not affect her despite the brutal nature of it. She had tried to get this done herself. The murders had released her from the evil that had surrounded her life. While she was in Rajan's house, she felt free.

She knew her place in the house but she knew that she was safe. She could not be independent but she began to think that she could be happy with her child. Happiness had been a dream for so long in her life. A smile appeared on her face. She was in a richer life now. She had a powerful secret now but she was not going to do anything to the people who had possibly given it to her.